MISSION SURVIVAL

GOLD OF THE
GODS

www.**missionsurvival**.co.uk

CHARACTER PROFILES

Beck Granger

At just thirteen years old, Beck Granger knows more about the art of survival than most military experts learn in a lifetime. When he was young he travelled with his parents to some of the most remote places in the world, from Antarctica to the African Bush, and he picked up many vital survival skills from the remote tribes he met along the way.

Uncle Al

Professor Sir Alan Granger is one of the world's most respected anthropologists. His stint as a judge on a reality television show made him a household name, but to Beck he will always be plain old Uncle Al – more comfortable in his lab with a microscope than hob-nobbing with the rich and famous. He believes that patience is a virtue and has a 'never-say-die' attitude to life. For the past few years he has been acting as guardian to Beck, who has come to think of him as a second father.

David & Melanie Granger

Beck's mum and dad were Special Operations Directors for the environmental direct action group, Green Force. Together with Beck, they spent time with remote tribes in some of the world's most extreme places. Several years ago their light plane mysteriously crashed in the jungle. Their bodies were never found and the cause of the accident remains unknown . . .

Marco & Christina de Castillo

These curly-haired twins live in Cartagena, a large city on the northern coast of Colombia. They like to tease their father, the mayor of the city, and can often be seen giggling together at private jokes. They are direct descendents of Don Gonzalo de Castillo, a famous conquistador who captained the first ship to sail to South America. Family legend says that he once discovered El Dorado – the legendary City of Gold .

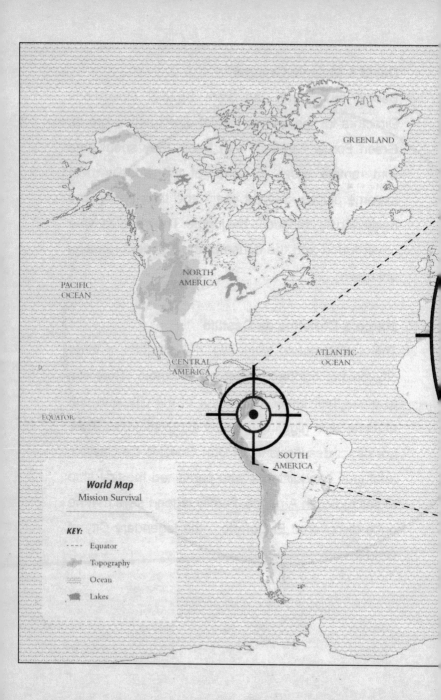

GREENLAND

PACIFIC
OCEAN

NORTH
AMERICA

ATLANTIC
OCEAN

CENTRAL
AMERICA

EQUATOR

SOUTH
AMERICA

World Map
Mission Survival

KEY:

- - - - Equator

Topography

Ocean

Lakes

ARCTIC OCEAN

CARTAGENA ●

BOGATÁ ★

COLOMBIA

EQUATOR

OCEANIA

SOUTH PACIFIC
OCEAN

ANTARCTICA

MISSION SURVIVAL

HAVE YOU READ THEM ALL?

GOLD OF THE GODS

Location: The Colombian Jungle

Dangers: Snakes; starvation; howler monkeys

Beck travels to Colombia in search of the legendary City of Gold. Could a mysterious amulet provide the key to uncovering a secret that was thought to be lost forever?

WAY OF THE WOLF

Location: The Alaskan Mountains

Dangers: Snow storms; wolves; white-water rapids

After his plane crashes in the Alaskan wilderness, Beck has to stave off hunger and the cold as he treks through the frozen mountains in search of help.

SANDS OF THE SCORPION

Location: The Sahara Desert

Dangers: Diamond smugglers; heatstroke; scorpions

Beck is forced into the Sahara Desert to escape a gang of diamond smugglers. Can he survive the heat and evade the smugglers as he makes his way back to safety?

TRACKS OF THE TIGER

Location: The Indonesian Wilderness

Dangers: Volcanoes; tigers; orang-utans

When a volcanic eruption strands him in the jungles of Indonesia, Beck must test his survival skills against red-hot lava, a gang of illegal loggers, and the tigers that are on his trail . . .

CLAWS OF THE CROCODILE

Location: The Australian Outback

Dangers: Flash floods; salt-water crocodiles; deadly radiation

Beck heads to the Outback in search of the truth about the plane crash that killed his parents. But somebody wants the secret to remain hidden – and they will kill to protect it.

GOLD OF THE GODS
A RED FOX BOOK 978 1 862 30479 6

First published in Great Britain by Red Fox
an imprint of Random House Children's Publishers UK
A Random House Group Company

This edition published 2008

18

Copyright © Bear Grylls, 2008
Written by Bear Grylls and Richard Madden
Cover artwork © Paul Carpenter, 2013
Map artwork © Ben Hasler, 2013

The Random House Group Limited supports The Forest Stewardship Council® (FSC®),
the leading international forest-certification organisation. Our books carrying the FSC
label are printed on FSC®-certified paper. FSC is the only forest-certification scheme
supported by the leading environmental organisations, including Greenpeace. Our
paper procurement policy can be found at www.randomhouse.co.uk/environment

MIX
Paper from
responsible sources
FSC® C016897

Set in Swiss 721 BT

RANDOM HOUSE CHILDREN'S PUBLISHERS UK
61–63 Uxbridge Road, London W5 5SA

www.**randomhousechildrens**.co.uk
www.**randomhouse**.co.uk

Addresses for companies within The Random House Group Limited can be found at:
www.randomhouse.co.uk/offices.htm

THE RANDOM HOUSE GROUP Limited Reg. No. 954009

A CIP catalogue record for this book is available from the British Library.

Printed and bound by CPI Group (UK) Ltd, Croydon, CR0 4YY

MISSION SURVIVAL

GOLD OF THE GODS

BEAR GRYLLS

RED FOX

*This book is for Marmaduke, my precious
middle son, and another apple of Papa's eye!
I hope you enjoy this and one day
we'll live such an adventure together.*

At last the rain had almost stopped. The rhythmic drumming on the jungle canopy far above had faded to a distant murmur. Only the sullen *drip, drip, drop* of water splashing into muddy pools disturbed the silence as a single shaft of sunlight broke through into the rainforest below.

Peering through the gloom, an inquisitive troop of howler monkeys clung to the lower branches of the trees. Their gaze followed the bright line of sunlight to where a bedraggled shape lay spread-eagled in a pool of light on the jungle floor. Every few minutes one let out a bloodcurdling bark and violently shook the branch on which it was sitting.

But the monkeys were beginning to lose interest in this strange hairless ape that lay so deathly still beneath them. This was no longer fun. When they had first begun hurling sticks down from the trees above, the hairless ape had tried to defend itself against the barrage of missiles. Once it had even barked back at them in their own language. But now it lay as unmoving as a lump of earth, no longer of interest. The time had come to move on.

As the noise of the monkeys slowly faded into the distance, a sigh that sounded almost human escaped from the inert form. Playing dead was not a survival strategy Beck Granger would normally use. Especially with a bumptious group of young howler monkeys. But with his body on the brink of exhaustion, he badly needed to look after what little energy he had left.

And somewhere not far off, a far worse threat still lurked. There was only one lord in the jungles of Colombia's Sierra Nevada mountains and it was not human. As night began to fall, the mighty jaguar, king of the jungle cats, would be patrolling his territory once more.

All day long the young teenager had felt his spirit stagger under the combined assault of rain and heat

2

and hunger. Drawing on every ounce of strength he still possessed, and using every shred of knowledge gleaned in a childhood spent learning the ways of survival, he had pushed himself onwards. Against all the odds he was still alive, and somewhere out there was the goal he was searching for.

In his fevered sleep he had come face to face with the Indian once more. He remembered the first time he had seen those gleaming eyes. How long ago it now seemed. The carnival. The twins. Don Gonzalo. That extraordinary night in the square. The start of the desperate quest to find the Lost City.

And then he remembered. Around his neck hung a muddied amulet in the shape of a golden toad, its eyes glistening in the sunlight, its mouth wide open. Adrenalin surged through Beck's veins. He still had one final chance.

Taking a long deep breath, he put the amulet to his lips.

And blew.

CHAPTER 1

Beck Granger strode onto the balcony of the five-star Hotel Casa Blanca and let out a low whistle. 'This,' he muttered under his breath, 'is unreal.' Cheered on by a boisterous crowd, an endless procession of carnival floats was flowing out of the narrow cobbled streets into the main square below.

Effigies of men with extravagant moustaches wearing doublets and ruffs swayed unsteadily above the crowd, while every few minutes a roar of approval went up as a particularly spectacular float came into view. Cartagena's annual carnival was in full swing and the strains of salsa, congo, rumba and Caribbean steel bands floated up on the breeze.

Behind Beck, in the ballroom from which he had just emerged, the scene could hardly have been more different. Elegantly dressed dignitaries chatted in small groups as waiters in starched whites passed silently between them. A four-piece string quartet was playing a jaunty waltz. Beck vaguely recognized the tune from his uncle's stodgy old classical music collection.

'Cool!' he muttered for the umpteenth time that day. Colombia was certainly a different country. It was also a different world. His mind spun back to the previous week. No more drizzly mornings trudging into breakfast along the school avenue. No more Mr Braintree and double maths for a whole month. And Mrs Armington (Armour Plating, as the boys always called her) would have to make do with screaming at the pigeons in the school quadrangle now that the boys had broken up for the Easter holidays. Beck's grin almost hurt.

'Beck! *Hola! Amigo!* '

Beck shook himself out of his daydream. The identical faces of two teenagers beamed mischievously back at him. The words had emerged simultaneously from under two matching mops of brown curls, high cheekbones and arching eyebrows. If it hadn't been for the huge gold rings dangling from the ears of the face on the right, he would have sworn he was seeing double.

'Marco. Christina. *Buenos días*.'

After just twenty-four hours in South America, Beck had already picked up a handful of useful Spanish phrases, but there was no danger yet of being mistaken for a local. Luckily the twins' English was a little more advanced. They had only met for the first time the previous day, when the twins and their father had greeted Beck and his uncle at the airport. Even so, he already felt like one of the family.

'I hope you're enjoying our little party, Señor Beck,' said Marco. 'That's such neat timing, you and your uncle coming to stay with us right now. Our carnival is the best – we Colombians know how to party. But come back inside – Dad is about to make his speech. Now we can find out what this is all about.'

'And the reason you and your uncle are both here,' added Christina. 'Isn't it a bit odd he hasn't told you why?'

'I've learned not to ask questions,' replied Beck wearily. 'Uncle Al tells me patience is a virtue. He likes to keep his projects secret during term time. So I don't get distracted from my school work. Or so he tells me.'

Christina led the way back into the ballroom, where the string quartet had stopped playing and a hush had fallen over the expectant crowd. Snaking their way through the guests, they made their way across the huge room. Beck saw that his uncle was chatting animatedly to a small group of VIPs. Judging by the half-empty champagne glass in one hand and the fat Cuban cigar in the other, he was enjoying being the centre of attention.

Now in his mid-sixties, Professor Sir Alan Granger was one of the world's most respected anthropologists. Over the years his studies of tribal peoples had become classic texts, compulsory reading for university students around the world. More recently his appearance on the judging panel of a TV reality show had made him a household name in the UK.

But to Beck he would always just be plain Uncle Al. More at home examining bits of charred bone at the bottom of a pit or fragments of parchment under a microscope than hobnobbing with the rich and famous.

Uncle Al had been Beck's guardian ever since that terrible day when the headmaster had sent for him and told him the dreadful news: Beck's parents were missing, presumed dead. Their light plane had crashed in the jungle, the wreckage spread for miles around. Their bodies had never been found and the reason for the plane crash never explained.

CHAPTER 2

Over the three years since the tragic death of his parents, Beck had grown very close to his Uncle Al and now thought of him like a second father. For months Beck had been inconsolable, but his Aunt Kathy and Uncle Al's never-say-die view of life – together with some terrific home cooking – had gradually revived his spirits.

Like most of the Granger family, Uncle Al had been a wanderer all his life. His work frequently took him to remote wildernesses around the world for months at a time, but whenever this coincided with the school holidays, he always invited Beck along. And on more than one occasion he'd had reason to be thankful for the teenager's survival skills.

Already, at the age of just thirteen, Beck knew

more about the art of survival than most military experts learned in a lifetime. David Granger, Beck's father, had been the Special Operations Director of Green Force, the environmental direct action group, and the family had lived with remote tribes in many of the world's most extreme places, from Antarctica to the African bush.

Just a few weeks before the end of term Beck had received an email sent by satellite phone from a remote location somewhere in the Amazon. Uncle Al had been invited by the Mayor of Cartagena to join him and his family for the Easter holidays in Colombia. A plane ticket had been booked and Beck was to fly out the day after term ended.

Beck guessed the invitation meant more than just a holiday in the sun, but Uncle Al had chosen not to explain. After spending a rainy afternoon in the school library locating Colombia on a map of South America and then scouring the Internet, Beck had finally tracked down some more information about the mysterious Mayor of Cartagena.

Mayor Rafael de Castillo, who he now knew better as the father of Marco and Christina, was the direct descendant of Don Gonzalo de Castillo, a famous conquistador. Gonzalo had sailed with Christopher Columbus on his voyages of discovery to the New World. He was famous as the founder of Cartagena, had become fabulously wealthy, and had died in mysterious circumstances after an expedition into the nearby Sierra Nevada mountains.

By now Beck and the twins had at last managed to squeeze their way to within a couple of metres of the podium at one end of the Hotel Casa Blanca's magnificent ballroom. As they jostled for a better view of the speakers, there was a squeal of feedback and the amplified rumble of someone clearing their throat.

'*Señoras y señores*,' boomed a disembodied voice.

A polite round of applause followed the introduction of the mayor, and the twins' father stepped up to the microphone. A tall man with dark, well-groomed hair, Don Rafael reminded Beck of an old-fashioned Hollywood star from the black and white era. Don Rafael was clearly an experienced public speaker. Every now and then a smile would break out on the faces of the guests, followed by an eruption of laughter around the room.

'He always tells that one,' Christina shouted into Beck's ear during one particularly loud outburst. 'Watch – he'll stroke his moustache now. He always does that when he's feeling pleased with himself.' Marco and Christina doubled up in a fit of giggles as Don Rafael duly obliged.

The crowd fell silent once more as the serious expression on the mayor's face indicated that he was reaching the climax of his speech. With a theatrical flourish of his arm, he gestured towards a huge oil painting hanging in an ornate gilt frame on the oak-panelled wall behind him. The subject of the portrait, a man roughly the same age as Don Rafael himself, was wearing doublet and hose and looking out from the battlements of a harbour wall. His right hand gestured towards a fleet of warships under full sail, their pennants fluttering in the breeze.

In a flash Beck realized who the subject of the portrait must be. As the twins' father struck up the same regal pose, the great conquistador Gonzalo de Castillo, founder of Cartagena, rose from beyond the grave. Once more the ballroom burst into spontaneous applause.

'Spot the family resemblance?' shouted Marco above the noise. 'I'd recognize that nose anywhere. Luckily Dad hasn't passed it on to us.'

'I hope he hasn't invited all these people here to tell them he fancies himself as a conquistador,' added Christina. 'That would be really embarrassing.'

As the applause died down once more, all eyes turned towards Uncle Al, who acknowledged his host and the crowd with a polite bow. Beneath the trademark eccentricity that the TV audience had found so endearing – a 'bumbling favourite uncle in a panama hat', as one critic had described him – was one of the sharpest brains of his generation.

Don Rafael was speaking quickly now and the silence of the audience and the expectant look on the faces around him reflected his enthusiasm. But it was only when the mayor uttered the words 'El Dorado' that Beck realized something out of the ordinary was in the air. The look on the twins' faces said it all as their mouths fell open in amazement. The mayor continued to address the gathering, his voice growing in excitement.

'My father thinks he knows where to find the Lost City,' whispered Marco, hardly able to breathe. 'It was found in the jungle by a small group of conquistadors under Gonzalo and then lost again for centuries. No one has ever known where to look. Until now.'

'And your uncle is here to help us find it,' added Christina. 'The expedition has been kept secret until now, but all the arrangements have been made and it will be ready to leave next week.'

'Welcome to Colombia, *amigo*!'

CHAPTER 3

A huge smile lit up Uncle Al's face as Beck and the twins tripped over themselves in their hurry to climb the steps onto the podium when the speeches had finished. Mayor Rafael was surrounded by an enthusiastic group of VIP guests, but Uncle Al could hardly wait to speak to the three excited teenagers.

'Keeping it all a secret from you was my toughest assignment so far, Beck, young man,' he said, grinning like a Cheshire cat. 'But my good friend Mayor Rafael insisted. They do things differently here. Walls have ears. Mum's the word and all that. Get my drift?' He tapped the side of his nose and raised an eyebrow at his nephew.

Out of the corner of his eye Beck could see the

twins staring at Uncle Al as if he had been speaking in Ancient Arabic.

'I hope you're taking us with you to find this Lost City, Uncle Al,' said Beck when at last he could get a word in edgeways. 'Sounds a lot more exciting than our last trip.' He and Uncle Al had set off into the wilderness together on what should have been a routine expedition to study the remains of the ancient Nubians of Sudan.

'Especially when it's the city that's lost rather than us,' he added archly.

'OK, OK, enough said, young man,' Uncle Al said hastily, winking at the twins. 'Can't win 'em all. Lost the plot. Lost us too. *Mea culpa. Dorkus maximus*, et cetera.'

'I hope these two young rascals are looking after you well, Beck,' said a booming voice with a thick Spanish accent. Mayor Rafael had extricated himself from the crowd of VIPs and was striding across the stage to join them. He towered over the twins as he proudly put an arm around each of them.

'They were just about to tell me about your ancestor Don Gonzalo and the Lost City, sir,' said

Beck, still a little overawed by the larger-than-life figure of Don Rafael. The mayor was dressed in his official uniform, sporting a bright purple sash and a hat that looked like it had last been worn by one of Gonzalo's conquistadors.

'Dad thinks he's Gonzalo, don't you, Dad?' said Marco.

'That's why he became mayor,' said Christina, smiling wickedly at her father. 'Just so he could dress up in funny clothes.' She paused and gave her father a nudge in his stomach.

'But Beck wants to know whether we can join the expedition to find the Lost City, don't you, Beck?' she went on, nodding frantically in Beck's direction.

'Well, no . . . I mean . . . well, actually, yes, sir,' stumbled Beck.

Just then a loud gong sounded, drowning out the mayor's reply. At the same time an officious-looking man in dark glasses and a peaked cap covered in gold braid appeared by the mayor's shoulder and whispered something in his ear. Beck noticed a long scar down one side of the man's face; his forehead was beaded with drops of sweat.

Mayor Rafael frowned slightly, as if the police-man's words had annoyed him, before breaking into a forced smile and speaking to Beck.

'It appears we must be moving on,' he said. 'Ramirez here says I must be ready to start the fire-works promptly at seven p.m. and we're already a little late. Your uncle and I need to . . . er . . . press the flesh, I think you English say. Beck, why don't you enjoy the carnival with the twins for a while and join us for the fireworks later?'

Leaving the mayor and Professor Granger with the sinister-looking Ramirez, Beck and the twins made their way out of the hotel into the scrum of carnival-goers. 'Follow us if you can,' bellowed Marco above the din. 'We're making for the church on the other side of the square. There's something you must look at. It will explain a lot about the Lost City – you'll see!'

The carnival was now in full swing and Beck abandoned himself to the ebb and flow of the huge crowd. At times he felt as if he had been tossed into the sea and was bobbing along like a cork on the waves. Everywhere he looked, magical sights caught his eye and his brain clicked and whirred like a camera on motordrive.

On stalls all around the square, street vendors were selling slices of sizzling meat cooked on hot bricks and wrapped in palm leaves. Piles of fruit lined the walkways and immaculately groomed white horses high-stepped elegantly past.

In the centre of the square a street performer, his face masked in white chalk and his lips the colour of cherries, was mingling with the crowd. He was a mime artist, silently copying the movements of unsuspecting passers-by. Beck laughed out loud as the man swayed his hips in time to an unsuspecting young señora in a polka-dot dress.

When the three teenagers finally reached the far side of the square, Beck looked up at the ornate façade of the Church of the Blessed Virgin. Its gold-painted spires glinted in the evening sunshine and a finely carved statue of the Madonna and Child gazed serenely down at them from an alcove above the giant wooden doors.

At the top of a sweeping stone staircase, Beck recognized the distinctive features of the conquistador, Don Gonzalo. The statue had clearly been copied from the oil painting hanging in the ballroom of the Hotel Casa Blanca.

'Don Gonzalo has the best view in the square,' laughed Christina. 'Dad once took a picture of me as a baby, sitting on his shoulders during the carnival. I'm not sure the old boy could manage my weight these days. His head would probably break off.'

'There are many legends about our ancestor,' said Marco. 'No one knows for sure what's true and what isn't. But we do know that in 1512 Gonzalo was the captain of the first ship to land in South America. Not far along the coast from here. The descriptions in the old books make it sound like paradise. Coconut palms and white sand stretching as far as the eye could see. The conquistadors probably wished they'd packed their surfboards. But somehow I don't think Don Gonzalo would have had much time for beach bums.'

'At first they thought the whole coast was uninhabited,' continued Christina, 'but then they found tracks in the forest and realized that there were people living here after all. The people we know today as the Kogi.'

'The who?' asked Beck.

'The Kogi,' Christina explained. 'They're an Indian tribe who live down the coast in the forests of the Sierra Nevada. A bit like the Maya and the Aztecs who Cortés discovered in Mexico. But the Kogi were never defeated by the conquistadors and they still live in the mountains, just like they did in the old days. We're taught about them in school, but we rarely see them. They're very shy and don't like to mix with the people in the towns.

'They knew how to make gold jewellery like the Aztecs,' Christina went on. 'But to them gold wasn't like money is for us. It was offered in sacrifice to their gods. They buried gold objects in the ground at their holy sites or threw them into holy lakes. That's where the conquistadors got the idea of "El Dorado", the City of Gold.'

CHAPTER 4

'So let's get this right,' said Beck, looking quizzically at the twins. 'Your great-great-great-great-great-grandfather, or there-abouts, arrived on the coast and went searching for El Dorado in the mountains where the Kogi Indians were living.'

Marco nodded and looked Beck straight in the eye. 'When Gonzalo found the city, he only had a few men with him, so he returned to Cartagena to mount another expedition. But before he could return, the Indians abandoned the city and changed the pathways through the jungle so Gonzalo was never able to find it again. He took his revenge by burning down one of the Kogi villages. He died soon after. Some say he was poisoned. But the only thing we know for sure is his last words.'

The twins pointed to a coat of arms carved into the plinth at the base of the statue of Don Gonzalo. Beck read out loud three words carved into the stone in an elaborate gothic script.

'*Perdido. No. Más*. What does that mean?'

'*Perdido no más*,' echoed Marco. 'The family motto. It means "Lost No More", but why Gonzalo said it when he couldn't find the Lost City again, nobody knows.'

'You say he was poisoned,' said Beck. 'Who by?'

'Maybe other conquistadors who wanted to find the gold from the Lost City. Perhaps even the Kogis. Some say he may have been under a Kogi curse. No one knows for sure,' replied Marco.

Beck's head was spinning as he tried to take in the twins' incredible story. Meanwhile more carnival floats were still arriving in the square. A giant effigy of Don Gonzalo was followed by a Spanish galleon under full sail. It was crewed by raven-haired beauty queens in sparkling bikinis hanging precariously from the masts, smiling and waving to the crowd.

Then a tidal wave of applause broke over the square. By far the biggest effigy Beck had seen so far was making its grand entrance. A giant papier-mâché toad painted a livid emerald green was being squeezed through a ceremonial arch into the square. But its bulbous mass was so huge, it quickly became wedged and could not be moved.

Volunteers standing nearby joined in an ungainly bout of pushing and shoving but were unable to shift it. Then, much to the crowd's amusement, a gang of Elvis look-alikes hurriedly dismounted from the float behind and started to manoeuvre it through sideways.

The toad finally burst into the square, its vast stomach sagging over the front of the float like a sumo wrestler's and its two huge legs straining under its bulk like immense balloons. The eyeballs bulging from the top of its head reminded Beck of the headlamps of an articulated lorry. 'Kermit, eat your heart out,' he muttered under his breath to no one in particular.

'There's also something else you should know,' Christina was saying, smiling broadly. Pointing down to where the toad was at last being pushed into pride of place in the centre of the square, she paused for effect. 'He's also on our coat of arms.'

'A giant toad?' said Beck. 'You'll be telling me Mickey Mouse had something to do with all this in a minute.'

'*La rana,* the toad, is an important part of the legend,' Christina explained. 'She's the fertility goddess of the Kogi Indians. The Kogis believe that if it weren't for her protection, all the gold from the Lost City would have been stolen. And then the jungle and the Kogis – in fact the whole world – would have come to an end. That's why both Gonzalo's effigy and the toad goddess form a central part of the carnival.'

'So the Lost City is more than just a Lost City for us,' added Marco. 'It's part of our family history too. That's why Dad wants to find it so much. And to do that he needs your uncle. Someone who understands the Indians and their culture. Otherwise he thinks he may suffer the same fate as Gonzalo.'

Beck's head was reeling. The closing fireworks display was due to begin in half an hour and there was no time for any more questions. Marco was already leading the way down into the crowd again so that they could take up their positions with the VIPs on the platform on the other side of the square.

'Stick close,' he shouted over his shoulder. 'We should just make it in time.'

Darkness was already falling and paraffin torches were being lit in preparation for the evening's entertainment. The crowd had become more raucous and Beck could smell *aguardiente*, the fiery local spirit, on the breaths of the more rowdy members. Shadows quivered and danced along the walls around the outside of the square.

And then Beck saw him. Or, to be more exact, he felt the man's eyes boring into him. It was as if a laser beam were being shone straight into his heart. The Indian was wearing a white woollen tunic and on his head was a pointed cap. Thick dark hair hung down to his shoulders in braids and his eyes were so bright that a light seemed to be shining behind them.

At first Beck thought that the man might be begging, but there was something in his bearing and the expression on his face, neither smiling or frowning, that was too dignified for that. And his eyes were so mesmerizing that for a moment Beck felt as if he were walking around inside his head and could read his thoughts. Beck was conscious now only of the rhythmic beating of the drums and the flickering shadows in the square. Suddenly, without ever once shifting his gaze, the Indian walked right up to him and whispered the words in his ear three times:

'*Perdido no más*.'

Then Beck passed out.

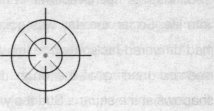

CHAPTER 5

Back on the balcony of the Hotel Casa Blanca, Chief of Police Pedro Ramirez was scanning the crowd in the square below. Behind a pair of aviator-style dark glasses favoured by security men and dictators the world over, his eyes darted restlessly back and forth.

Not for nothing did his men know him as *El Reptil*, the Reptile. They said that his cold eyes never missed a trick. Some even joked that he had never been known to blink. But for the head of security for Cartagena, the day of the annual carnival was no different from any other. This was a day of work, not play.

Scanning the rooftops with an expert eye, he carefully noted the positions of his men as, every few seconds, the micro-receiver in his left ear crackled into life. So far, the day was going well. The mayor had delivered his speech to the VIPs and the crowd seemed good-natured enough, despite a few rowdy local ruffians looking a little the worse for wear.

Ramirez's reputation for ruthless efficiency and iron discipline had been earned the hard way, and he was not about to throw it away now. On his watch, all would go according to plan. And with news of the expedition to the Lost City spreading through the crowd like wildfire, he was taking no chances.

Everything had proceeded like clockwork. Mayor Rafael had kept his speech short, as requested. And if he had not, one of Ramirez's men had been positioned next to the sound engineer to cut the microphone feed on a prearranged signal. The VIPs had moved from the ballroom onto the platform outside with the minimum of fuss. When it came to the smooth running of public events, no one was in any doubt who ran the show. And it wasn't Mayor Rafael.

But all this was the easy bit. Now that the light

was beginning to fade and the crowd was growing more animated, keeping control of any disturbance would be more of a problem. And this year, of all years, Ramirez had reason to be nervous.

As he was turning to leave the balcony and join the VIPs on the stage below, a commotion in the crowd made him stop. To his annoyance his view was blocked by the bloated figure of the toad, whose bulbous eyes and grinning mouth seemed to leer mockingly back at him.

Ramirez cursed and reached for his radio. *'Qué pasa?'* he barked.

A storm of white noise exploded in his ear. Ramirez listened intently. He could see two of his men peering into the crowd through high-powered binoculars from the roof of the church opposite. In the shadows of the bell tower, a high-velocity rifle with telescopic sights was brought into the firing position.

Ramirez smiled. His men had been well trained. But then, of course, he knew that already. Chief of Police Pedro Ramirez had not been the commandant of the National Police Training Centre in Bogotá for five years for nothing. The men under his command were not only hand-picked. They were also hand-trained.

As the gabble in his ear subsided, Ramirez relaxed. When Beck had passed out, it had caused a commotion in the tightly packed crowd, and in the confusion a scuffle had broken out. The disturbance had calmed down as quickly as it had started. The rifle withdrew again inside the shadows of the bell tower.

On the viewing platform below, oblivious to any problem, Mayor Rafael and his guests were preparing for the climax of the carnival. 'You have fireworks displays for your Señor Fawkes, Professor Granger?' the mayor was asking his distinguished guest. 'But only for Señor Fawkes. I am right, no? In Colombia we celebrate with fireworks many days of the year. But for our carnival here in Cartagena, we like the biggest. *El óptimo!* The very best. You shall soon see.'

The mayor stood up to a roar of approval from the crowd, which he acknowledged with a statesman-like bow before making his way forward to a cluster of microphones at the front of the stage. Uncle Al listened with a polite smile to a speech that sounded much like the one he had just heard in the ballroom of the Hotel Casa Blanca. Only this time there was no mention of the Lost City. To the mayor's evident delight, once again the crowd laughed in all the right places.

As Don Rafael turned to introduce this year's guest of honour with a regal flourish, Professor Granger recognized the words '*pirata inglés*' ('English pirate'). Caught off guard, he raised his panama hat and gave a nervous wave to the crowd, unsure what the mayor had been saying.

Then the penny dropped. It was clear Mayor Rafael had a wicked sense of humour. Sir Francis Drake, the conqueror of the Spanish Armada, had stormed the city in 1586. In exchange for mercy, a huge ransom had been paid, and to this day all Englishmen were considered pirates. But judging by the reaction of the crowd, there were no hard feelings. Alan Granger breathed a sigh of relief.

As the mayor's speech ended, mayhem was finally let loose in the night sky. Star bursts and flares exploded in a barrage of sound. Fire fountains bathed the crowd in rainbows of coloured light; they screamed and cheered in approval.

Caught in the crush in the centre of the square, Beck was at last coming to his senses after his encounter with the Indian. He felt himself being shaken, and a voice he dimly recognized was yelling in his ear, 'Beck. Beck. What happened? Are you all right?' The voice wavered and echoed, as if someone were shouting down at him from the top of a well.

Beck struggled to remember where he was. Loud bangs exploded all around him and a mad artist seemed to be chucking tins of paint around inside his skull. Then, in a flash, it came back to him. Cartagena. The twins. The carnival. The Indian with the gleaming eyes.

Beck slowly sat up and looked around. The blood had drained from his normally ruddy features and his tousled brown hair was even more ruffled than usual.

CHAPTER 6

'Beck, Beck. Are you all right? What happened? You look like you've seen a ghost.' He recognized Christina's voice as Marco helped him to his feet.

'What happened to the Indian?' muttered Beck. 'The Indian with the strange eyes. Surely you must have seen him?' He described the man he had seen in the crowd. He could picture him again now in his mind's eye – his white tunic, thick, dark eyebrows framing the glittering eyes.

Christina listened intently, her mouth dropping open in disbelief as Beck described the man he had seen. 'Beck, the man you describe is a Kogi. You remember. The tribe who live in the forest of the Sierra Nevada, where the Lost City was found by Don Gonzalo.'

'Yes,' said Marco, solemnly voicing his sister's unspoken thoughts. 'But there were no Kogis in the crowd today, Beck. The Mamas, their holy men, forbid it. You must have been dreaming it. You have a vivid imagination, my friend.'

'But I saw him – and he spoke to me . . . Yes, I remember now. *Perdido no más*. He said it three times. That's Gonzalo's motto, isn't it? "Lost no more".'

Marco's answer was drowned out by a volley of bangs and flashes as a barrage of fireworks exploded overhead. The Grand Parade that marked the finale of the carnival had begun and the floats were being paraded in front of the VIP platform. The teenagers could see the mayor clapping and waving like a man possessed.

'This is Dad's big moment,' shouted Christina. The effigy of Don Gonzalo was making its way unsteadily towards the stage. Accompanied by a guard of conquistadors, it waved drunkenly to the crowd as it rocked from side to side. When it came alongside, the mayor rose and signalled to Professor Granger to climb aboard. The two beauty queens Beck had seen earlier greeted the men with a kiss on each cheek and placed garlands of flowers around their necks.

'Quick,' yelled Marco. 'We're near Gonzalo's Arch, where the parade leaves the square. If we hurry, we can watch the floats go by.'

Still feeling slightly unsteady on his feet, Beck followed the twins as they snaked through the crush to where a group of Ramirez's men were hemming the crowd in with ropes on both sides of the route to the arch.

'That's odd,' said Christina in Beck's ear. 'I've never seen the crowd kept away from the floats before. Ramirez has gone power crazy. I wish he'd just let everyone have some fun.' Beck looked at her blankly. 'He was that goon in the uniform who was talking to Dad in the ballroom just now,' she added. 'He's chief of police in Cartagena. Likes to think he runs the place.'

Beyond the cordon of policemen, Beck could see the horses pulling Gonzalo's float snort nervously and paw the ground. They rolled their eyes as the bang and fizz of the explosions from the fireworks rocked the square. The two conquistadors holding the horses' heads were talking into earpieces and seemed to be nodding at the police.

As Gonzalo's float passed by, they heard something that sounded like a tin can bouncing over the cobbles. It was followed by a muffled bang as clouds of dense smoke engulfed the crowd. Immediately the police closed in around them, pushing the crowd back towards the middle of the square.

'Marco, Christina! Get down! Get down!' Beck shouted, pulling the twins to the ground. 'Something's wrong. That smoke isn't from a firework.'

By now Ramirez's men were swarming everywhere and panic began to spread through the crowd. A series of loud bangs echoed around the buildings and Beck could see rifles appearing from behind balustrades on the roofs. A deep *whop whop whop* of helicopter blades descended from the sky above.

'*Estúpido!*' spluttered Marco. 'That idiot Ramirez is guaranteed to make things worse. That chopper is blowing all the smoke down onto the crowd.'

'Follow me,' Beck shouted as they forced their way through the crowd in the direction of the arch, where the swirling cloud of green smoke seemed thinnest. At last, crouched down again, he could breathe in fresh air.

'Look. Over here!' said Marco. 'I can see under the smoke. They're trying to rescue Dad and Professor Granger. There's a car and . . .' His voice tailed off as the telltale rattle of a second canister bouncing along the cobbles was immediately followed by a *phutt* and a loud hiss; more clouds of dense smoke engulfed them.

But Beck had already seen enough. Just before the second canister exploded, he had caught a glimpse of something that made his heart freeze. The float carrying the effigy of Don Gonzalo had come to a halt just beyond the arch. A black limousine with tinted windows was blocking its path and the conquistadors were shouting and waving their arms wildly.

But instead of swords, they were now brandishing pistols and shouting at the mayor and Professor Granger, who were being bundled roughly off the float. The doors on the near side of the limo were pulled open and the pair pushed roughly inside.

As smoke engulfed the crowd once more, the salsa music pumping out of the PA system was turned off and Marco recognized the voice of the chief of police appealing for calm. Then, from beyond the arch, came a high-pitched squeal of tyres. The crowd began to break up in confusion.

Beck's brain was working overtime. A switch had been thrown in his mind and instinct had taken over. If they crouched close to the ground, they would still be able to breathe while the panicking crowd dispersed. He gestured to the twins to stay low, then covered his mouth and peered towards the arch, his eyes stinging badly and the screams of the crowd ringing in his ears.

After what seemed like an age the smoke began to thin. The three teenagers stared in horror towards the float beyond the arch. The black limo was no longer to be seen. The effigy of Don Gonzalo, its arms still waving, lay on the cobbles, grinning amiably towards the sky. Two bouquets of flowers lay tossed aside on the cobblestones and petals floated gently to the ground in the night air. A panama hat had come to rest at a jaunty angle in the gutter.

But the mayor and Professor Granger were gone.

CHAPTER 7

Beck's dreams that night were troubled. Once more he was back in the square. The Indian with the glittering eyes was pointing at the sky, where the jungles of the Sierra Nevada seemed to hover in the clouds. But each time Beck tried to move, a giant wave crashed down on him, flooding the square.

And then the crowd turned into huge shoals of fish darting back and forth. Chasing them this way and that, the carnival effigies had become sharks with bared teeth and staring eyes. And Don Gonzalo, his mouth leering in a ghastly grin, his teeth jagged, was no longer chasing the fish. It was Beck he was after now.

Lungs bursting, fighting for air, Beck struck out

desperately towards the sky. Somewhere above him he could hear the dull sound of the church bell ringing above the waves. He could see the spire clearly above the surface, shining in the bright sunlight. If only he could escape those vicious teeth. If only he could reach the surface before they ripped into the soft flesh of his legs. If only—

Beck sat bolt upright in his bed. Wide awake now, he struggled to remember where he was. The ringing had stopped and somewhere downstairs he could hear someone speaking.

'Pronto?'

Beck recognized Marco's voice talking into the phone in the hall below. At once the dramatic events of the previous evening came flooding back. With a sick feeling in the pit of his stomach, he could see the smoke canisters exploding around him and the chaos erupting in the square. Then the frightening truth hit home once again. Uncle Al and Mayor Rafael had been kidnapped. Beck had heard about Colombia's reputation as the 'Kidnap Capital of the World' and his heart sank. Almost certainly the gang would demand a large ransom in return for the safe return of Uncle Al and the mayor.

The previous night, in a blur of flashing blue lights, squealing tyres and blaring horns, Ramirez's men had spirited the three teenagers out of the square. Still reeling from the shock, they were soon back in the safety of the mayor's hacienda a few kilometres down the coast. Beck was relieved to see a three-metre-high chain-mail fence surrounding the grounds.

Doña Maria de Castillo, the twins' mother and the head of an international aid agency, was away on a field trip in a remote part of Africa. Making contact with her was proving difficult and no one knew when she was likely to return. Meanwhile Señora Cordova, the housekeeper, clucked around them, cooking supper and telling anyone who would listen that everything would be fine.

Police Chief Ramirez was at his oily worst. Nervously running a finger up and down the scar in his hollow cheek, he fixed his thin lips in a permanent sneer. The twins listened in surly silence, clearly unimpressed by Ramirez's promise that his team were doing everything they could to track down the kidnappers.

'If they're that good, why couldn't they have stopped the gang in the first place?' said Marco later as they dragged themselves despondently to bed.

Now, in the cold light of morning, Beck held his breath and listened intently. Marco was evidently talking to Ramirez, who was giving him an update on the latest information. From the tone of Marco's voice, Beck guessed that the news was not good.

Hurriedly pulling on some clothes, he made his way along the balcony, glancing into Christina's room as he passed. Everything was neat and tidy. In pride of place on the wall above the bed was a framed photograph of the Colombian pop star, Shakira. Beck couldn't help noticing that it had been signed in person and wondered how many more pop stars were on first-name terms with the twins.

In Marco's room, the contrast could hardly have been greater. A hurricane looked like it had ripped through overnight and clothes lay scattered around the floor in untidy piles. A poster of the Colombian football team, also signed, had been Blu-tacked unevenly to the wall. One corner had come loose and was curling downwards at an awkward angle.

Down in the hallway at the foot of a sweeping wooden staircase that creaked loudly as he descended, Marco and Christina were already deep in conversation.

'Ramirez says there is nothing he can do until the gang contact him with their demands,' Marco was saying. 'He's put a police guard on the house in case the gang try to kidnap us as well. We are forbidden to leave under any circumstances. The Reptile says it's for our own safety.'

'What he means is he doesn't want us poking our noses in where they're not wanted,' said Christina with a contemptuous toss of her curls.

Beck took in this latest development. 'We can't just sit on our backsides and do nothing,' he said after a while. 'Anyway, it might not be money the gang want. Surely it must be something to do with the expedition to the Lost City. Why else would they have kidnapped the mayor and Uncle Al just after the announcement?'

'Ramirez didn't want my father to make that announcement,' said Marco. 'He said it was too dangerous.'

'But the gang must have already known about the expedition,' said Christina. 'It must have leaked out somehow. Ramirez probably couldn't keep his mouth shut and told some of his goons. The walls have ears in Colombia.'

'But even your father doesn't know exactly where the city is,' said Beck. 'After all, it wouldn't be the *Lost* City if he did.'

'Yes, but maybe the gang thinks he knows how to find it, and with Professor Granger's expert knowledge of the Indians, they could force them to take them there,' suggested Marco.

'And loot the gold before the archaeologists get there,' added Christina. A silence fell on the room as this possibility sank in.

'Do you think your dad may have known more than he was letting on?' asked Beck finally.

'I overheard him once telling Mum he was

convinced Gonzalo made a map before he died, but no one in the family has ever found it.' Marco paused and looked across at his sister, as if for reassurance. Christina gave a brief nod. 'Come with us, Beck,' he said quietly. 'There's something you should see.'

CHAPTER 8

The twins led the way along an oak-panelled corridor before stopping in front of a polished door with a brass plaque on it. The single word, *Jefe*, had been etched on the plaque in a flowery copperplate. 'Hail to the Chief,' said Christina, raising her eyebrows knowingly at Beck.

Marco went into his father's study and reappeared moments later, clutching a heavy, ancient key that looked to Beck as if it had been used to lock up prisoners in the Tower of London. Hanging next to it on a rusty key ring was another key that looked like a miniature version of its larger brother.

Further down the corridor, Marco led the way through a door. The hacienda had been built in the old Spanish style around a stone courtyard. In the centre was an intricately carved fountain of a dolphin and on the far side was an ancient wooden door that looked like it hadn't been opened for many years.

'Dad always keeps it locked and no one is allowed in,' said Marco. 'The old part of the hacienda was built by Gonzalo himself, using beams from the galleon he sailed in from Spain. It's like stepping back into history.'

Marco slowly inserted the larger of the two keys into the lock. There was a flinty sound like a rusty bicycle chain as the key turned with a rough jolt. Marco pushed and the door creaked open on its ancient hinges. Shafts of early morning sun lit up the interior of the room in a swirl of dust. Inside, a long wooden table was surrounded by carved high-backed chairs. Five brass candlesticks covered in dribbling waterfalls of melted wax stood in a line along the centre of the table.

Hanging from the beams were the everyday objects of a Spanish warship. A musket, its butt almost entirely rotted away, was displayed next to a curved rapier with moth-eaten tassels still attached to the scabbard. On an oak-panelled wall at the far end of the room hung a ship's wheel.

'The table was taken from the map room in Gonzalo's flagship,' said Marco. 'We think Columbus himself may have sat around it on these very chairs. There are many legends surrounding Gonzalo. When we were younger, we were very frightened of this room. My family have always believed that Gonzalo was sitting in the chair at the head of the table on the night he died.' He paused. 'It's also said that anyone who sits in that chair will find the Lost City . . .' Marco's voice trailed off.

'Or die trying.' Christina was standing silently behind Beck and her voice made him jump. 'Dad never allows anyone to come in here except on very special occasions. And as far as we know, he's never sat in the chair.'

'Until perhaps a few days ago.' Marco's face was stern now and he looked worried. 'The day before you and your uncle arrived in fact. Dad was muttering our family motto all day. I asked him about it and he told me he had been into Gonzalo's room – he was sure there was some kind of puzzle or a clue. But he wouldn't say what.'

'Do you think the map to the Lost City may be hidden in this room then?' asked Beck.

'It's not possible,' replied Marco. 'Every inch has been searched many times, even under the floorboards and behind the panels. Dad badly wanted to find it but he never could.'

Beck walked slowly into the room and made his way towards Gonzalo's chair. His heart was beating fast now. As a child he had been taught not to believe in ghosts or superstitions or tales of Bluebeard and things that went bump in the night.

'Poppycock,' Uncle Al had once told him. 'All poppycock.' And Beck was inclined to agree. Although these days he used a different, rather ruder, word to describe it himself. In the school dormitory when he was a new boy, he had realized at once that it was one of the older boys making tapping noises to scare the 'piglets', as the juniors were known.

Once he had got himself into serious hot water when he tried to turn the tables after lights out one

56

night: covered in a sheet, he'd leaped out at one of the seniors, making screeching banshee noises. Just his luck it happened to be the Head of House. Bentley, or Bent Jaw, as he was known, had chosen not to see the funny side and Beck had spent the following two Saturdays in detention.

But now Beck was pacing boldly across the room, the ancient floorboards creaking ominously under his feet. His eyes flicked ceaselessly back and forth. As a young child he had spent time in the bush with the Masai in Kenya and he had learned how to use his eyes to survive. Now it was pure instinct. On the mantelpiece above the fireplace he saw a scattering of ancient coins and the tattered remains of an old flag.

Finally he came to a halt behind Gonzalo's chair, placing the palms of his hands on its high back. Then, without warning, he pulled the chair out from under the table. And sat down. A jolt like an electric shock surged through his body as Christina let out a yelp of surprise.

CHAPTER 9

It was at that very moment that Beck saw it. Above the fireplace directly opposite his chair hung an oil painting of Don Gonzalo. By now Beck recognized the conquistador's features as if they were his own. No one could mistake the goatee beard or the long face with its distinctive Roman nose.

But it was not these that caught his attention now. Beck's eagle eyes had noted them the moment he entered the room. It was Don Gonzalo's pointing finger and the direction in which his eyes were gazing that made his heart knock against his ribs. From his position in the chair, and only from the exact position where he was now sitting, he could see that both the finger and Don Gonzalo's eyes were pointing directly at the words under the family crest on the ornate gilt frame.

'*Perdido no más*.' Beck whispered the words as if in a trance. 'That's it. That's the clue. Your father was staring right at it all the time and never realized.'

Mystified, the twins followed Beck's gaze across the room and stared blankly at the painting of Gonzalo.

'Look. Follow his finger directly up.' Beck traced a straight line through the air from the top of Gonzalo's finger towards the top of the portrait where it bordered the frame. 'His eyes are looking at your family motto. But his finger is pointing directly at the letter O.'

In an instant Marco had dashed around the table and was lifting the dusty old portrait down from the wall. Laying it flat on the table, the three teenagers stared down at the embossed wooden crest of *la rana*, the toad, and the family motto beneath.

'And the letter O is different to all the other letters,' whispered Christina, finishing Beck's sentence. 'It seems to be covered by some sort of flap.'

'And that's because it's actually a keyhole,' said

Beck, pushing a fingernail into the curve on the outer side of the carved O. There was a click as the central portion of the O slid back. Beneath was the unmistakable outline of a keyhole.

'The other key. It's the lock for the other key,' murmured Marco. 'Beck, you're a genius. And not one of us ever saw it. We never knew what this key was for and it was in front of us all along. We were all so scared of the curse, we never dared to sit in Gonzalo's chair. That's what he's been trying to tell us all along.'

Marco grappled with the smaller key and, with shaking hands, inserted it into the lock. And turned. As if by magic, the belly of the toad on the embossed crest swung open. Beck blinked in astonishment. In front of them lay a golden amulet. It had been made in the shape of a toad, just like the one on the family's coat of arms. Its stomach bulged and its eyes glowed green in the dim light while its mouth gaped wide open.

Christina picked up the amulet on its gold chain and dangled it in front of them. '*La rana*,' said Marco in disbelief. 'The legend we were told as children.

The toad will appear when the Lost City is found.'

But Beck's attention had shifted to a folded parchment that still lay in a delicately carved recess at the back of the secret compartment. The words *Mapa Ciudad de Los Koguis* were still clearly visible in a copybook italic script.

'Map of the City of the Kogis,' said Beck, his voice breaking with excitement. 'This is what your dad was looking for all along. But he must have decided to hunt for the Lost City without the map . . .'

'. . . and the kidnappers must have thought he had discovered it,' said Marco, finishing Beck's sentence. 'And now they want to find the Lost City and loot the gold.'

'So at last it all makes sense,' whispered Christina in a trance, her head swaying gently in time with the golden frog. '*Perdido no más*.'

'*Perdido no más*,' echoed Beck. 'Lost no more. The Lost City is lost no more!'

CHAPTER 10

Huddled over Gonzalo's table, Beck and the twins peered down at the ancient piece of parchment in awed silence. At first glance it hardly looked like a map at all. Lines, crosses, circles and numbers tumbled across the page as if the mapmaker had been grappling with a complex set of mathematical equations rather than the location of a Lost City.

In the bottom right-hand corner was a circle with a cross roughly drawn across it. 'Compass rose,' said Beck, stabbing his finger at the map. 'Well, at least we know which way we're facing. These old maps were very basic – the conquistadors had no reliable instruments for plotting their position.' Beck remembered his time with the Tao tribe in the South Pacific, learning to navigate with the stars.

'Some of these numbers must be nautical miles and I think it's divided into sections. This bit here must be the coastline, roughly where we are now. Look, here!' He pointed to where the word *Cart* had been written next to the rough outline of a castle. 'This must be Cartagena. And this' – he pointed to a miniature symbol of a Spanish galleon further along the coast – 'must be where they landed when they found the city the first time.'

Along the bottom of the map was a signature that reminded Beck of a document signed by Queen Elizabeth I he had once seen in a history book at school. Above a series of florid curves and flourishes were the words *Gonzalo de Castillo* with *Año de Nuestro Señor* written in smaller letters underneath, followed by some Roman numerals: MDXXII.

'Fifteen . . . twenty . . . two,' stumbled Christina, peering hard at the numbers. 'I knew those boring Latin lessons would come in handy one day. That was the year of Gonzalo's death. He must have hidden this map not long before he died.'

'Or was murdered, like the legend says,' muttered Marco darkly.

His words were interrupted by the sound of a bell clanging in the courtyard outside. The teenagers jumped guiltily, as if they had been caught red-handed in the middle of a bank robbery.

'Quick,' said Marco. 'There's someone at the front door of the hacienda. We mustn't let anyone see the map or the amulet.' Beck quickly folded the parchment and slid it into his back pocket, then hung the amulet of the toad around his neck and tucked it under his shirt as Marco and Christina replaced Gonzalo's portrait on the wall.

Marco led the way back across the courtyard and along the corridor towards the main entrance of the house. Through the stained glass of the front door they could see the flashing blue lights of police cars and the familiar outline of the peaked cap of an officer of the Colombian police force. Señora Cordova was already at the door.

Ramirez was in no mood for pleasantries as he strode past Marco into the hall. The harsh *click-clack* of his leather boots on the flagstones echoed loudly around the walls. He was greeted by a screech and the sound of flapping wings. Beck looked up to the balcony, where the family's pet parakeet was hopping from leg to leg on the banister, cocking a nervous eye at this unwelcome intruder.

Ramirez stared up at the bird with an expression of ill-disguised malice. Señora Ramirez was an expert cook and would surely know a tasty recipe for stuffed roast parakeet.

He spun round to address the three teenagers. '*Buenos días, amigos*,' he said, before launching into a volley of quick-fire Spanish. Gone was the oily mask of concern of the previous evening, when he had escorted them back to the hacienda. Today it had been replaced by impatience verging on rudeness.

Expressions of disbelief and anger flitted like dark shadows across the faces of the twins. Beck recognized only one word of the policeman's speech. But it was enough to make his heart freeze. The horrified look on the twins' faces confirmed his worst fears. Señora Cordova gasped.

There was a brief silence as Ramirez let the impact of his words sink in. When he continued, it was in short bursts, as if he were giving orders.

Marco nodded sullenly and shot brief glances at his sister, who was still staring at Ramirez in disbelief.

And then, as suddenly as he had arrived, Ramirez was gone. Outside, a flunky saluted and opened the door of a police car bearing the crest of the Chief of Police of Cartagena. Ramirez sank into the comfortable leather seat before barking an instruction at the driver. In the distance Beck saw the electric gates swing open and a pair of armed guards saluted and stood to attention.

The single word still echoed in his brain.

'*Narcotráficantes*,' repeated Marco, reading Beck's mind. 'Drug traffickers.'

CHAPTER 11

'Ramirez says he thinks Dad and Professor Granger have been kidnapped by one of the drug cartels,' explained Christina in a stunned monotone. She let out a long groan and put her head in her hands. 'I'm just so worried about them.'

Marco shook his head and took a deep breath. 'Ramirez says it's more important than ever that we don't leave the hacienda. He says it's for our own safety. All calls to the hacienda have been diverted to police HQ. There's an armed guard on the gate. Basically, we're prisoners too.'

The horrified silence was broken only by the eerie cawing of birds in the palm trees outside the window. After what felt like an age, Beck broke the spell. 'We've got to do something. We can't just sit on our butts and let this happen to Uncle Al and Mayor Rafael. What if Ramirez is wrong and the gang *are* more interested in looting the gold from the Lost City? Why don't we just give Ramirez the map? Then the police can get there first and ambush the gang when they arrive.'

'It's too risky,' Christina insisted with a toss of her curls. 'And anyway, Dad hates Ramirez. He says he's a trigger-happy fool. No one trusts him. He'd probably end up killing them, not saving them.'

'But now that we have the map, *we* must at least try,' said Beck. 'We owe it to Uncle Al and your father. If we can't trust the police, then we'll just have to find the Lost City ourselves. Surely there must be some way out of here?'

'There's chain-mail fencing all the way round the grounds on three sides, right the way down to the sea,' replied Christina. 'We could always fly. Got any other good ideas?' Her eyes were turning red and watery. Marco stretched out an arm to comfort her but was brushed irritably aside.

Beck was too wrapped up in his own thoughts to pay attention. 'I'm telling you, we can get away from here without Ramirez noticing. He's a goon, Christina. You know that better than anyone.' He paused. 'Come with me, guys,' he said after a while. 'I've got an idea . . .'

Beck led the way into the formal dining room at the front of the house. Early morning sunlight was streaming through the French windows that opened out onto a terrace, from where steps led down to a manicured lawn. Beck walked over to a glass display case. 'It was one of the first things I noticed when we arrived,' he said. 'I just couldn't keep my eyes off it. I think it's one of the most beautiful things I've ever seen. It's also given me an idea.'

'It's gold filigree work,' said Christina, opening the top of the glass case. Inside lay a delicate gold object on a bed of blue velvet. 'Dad forbids us ever to touch it because it's so valuable.'

In front of them lay a miniature model of a raft. Matchstick men stood on a square platform of logs lashed together with rope. One held a tiller while another brandished a spear and gazed over the side into the sea of blue velvet. On the mast a rect-angular sail was operated by two gold braids.

'It's like a spider's web made with gold fibres,' said Christina. 'It belonged to Gonzalo. We think it was made by the Indians who lived in the Lost City. The Kogi people we told you about who still live in the jungle. Remember?' She paused. 'Like the Indian man you thought you saw in the square last night.'

A flicker of pain passed over Beck's face as the memory returned. The man's eyes still burned brightly in his memory, but now even he was beginning to think he had just imagined the Indian in the heat and the chaos. And anyway, his mind was on other things now. The garden of the hacienda was surrounded by a fence all the way down to the sea . . . Surely Ramirez's men would not look for them there.

Marco's voice broke through his thoughts. 'When Gonzalo arrived in South America, the first time they saw the Indians was on the sea. The Spanish cronistas – historians – made drawings of the rafts they used. They looked almost identical to this one.'

Beck studied the raft closely, screwing up his

eyes as he inspected the delicate gold web. 'Time for a walk,' he said suddenly.

The twins followed as Beck led the way onto the terrace. The scent of ripe peaches hung in the morning air like perfume. On the far side of the lawn, the jungle that surrounded the hacienda on three sides closed in again – the fence that ran around the grounds was out of sight from here, buried in the undergrowth. As they made their way along a path skirting the jungle, tendrils hanging from the branches of the huge trees brushed past them like the tentacles of giant jellyfish.

They soon found themselves in a grove of tall palm trees, where the undergrowth gave way to sand, and saw that they had reached a small bay. White spume seethed and bubbled on the shore, where a steady stream of rollers was breaking.

'There's only one way out of here without being noticed,' said Beck as they stared out towards the horizon. 'And that's by sea. If we can build a raft like the one the Indians used, we can sail down the coast. That's how Gonzalo found the Lost City, so why shouldn't we?

'You can see on the map that it's in the mountains not far from the coast. If we're lucky, we'll find it before the kidnappers. Then we'll have the element of surprise. If we sail tonight after it gets dark, by the time Ramirez works out we've gone we'll be miles away down the coast.'

Beck had only just stopped speaking when, from somewhere behind them, there was a rustle of leaves in the bushes. For the second time that morning, his blood ran cold.

A familiar voice broke the silence.

'*Buenos días, amigos*,' said Ramirez.

CHAPTER 12

Beck's heart sank as the awful truth dawned. Hiding in the undergrowth, following them just out of sight, Ramirez the Reptile had tricked them into revealing their plan to sail down the coast and find the Lost City. Their only chance of rescuing Uncle Al and the twins' father was now gone.

Drawing himself up to his full height, Beck turned to confront the police chief with a frosty glare. He was greeted by a loud screech from behind the bushes, followed by a burst of hysterical laughter. Marco and Christina were shaking uncontrollably, tears rolling down their cheeks.

'Will someone please explain—?' began Beck.

'*Buenos días, amigos*,' spat Ramirez for the second time. His words were greeted with a renewed explosion of mirth as Marco and Christina doubled up once more.

'Ringo! Stop that, Ringo!' shouted Christina as she disappeared behind the bushes.

Beck looked on in amazement, hardly able to speak. 'Will someone please—?' he began again as Christina reappeared, clutching a flapping mass of brightly coloured feathers that squawked loudly, while every few seconds pecking at her earrings with sudden darts of his head.

'Señor Beck,' said Marco in a pompous voice, as if they were in the presence of royalty. 'May I introduce Don Ringo the Gringo.'

'Otherwise know as plain Ringo the wicked parakeet,' added Christina. 'Dad called him Ringo because beetles are his favourite food' – she shook her head with a despairing look – 'which he thinks is very funny. When he was young, Dad was a sailor on a ship that visited Liverpool and he met John, Paul, George . . .'

'And Ringo,' said Marco as the parakeet jumped from Christina's arm onto his shoulder while directing an inquisitive eye at Beck. 'Ringo was Dad's favourite. He said he never stopped cracking jokes . . .' He paused and gave Ringo a sideways glare. 'Which I guess explains every-thing.'

'Bingo!' exclaimed Beck, a huge smile lighting up his face.

'No, Beck, *Ringo*,' said Christina, trying unsuccessfully to hide her impatience. 'You know, the pop—'

But Beck wasn't listening. 'Balsa,' he said, pointing excitedly into the distance. 'That tree over there. The really tall one. It's a balsa tree. That's what the Indians used to build rafts like the one in Gonzalo's model. We've got all the materials we need to build the real thing right here. And unless we get away tonight' – he glared at Ringo – 'it really will be Ramirez jumping out at us from behind the bushes.'

Beck led the way through the undergrowth. 'You can tell they're balsa trees by the flowers on the ends of the branches. They look like ice-cream cones.' He pointed up at the smooth white bark of the trunk, which rose straight as an arrow towards the sky. 'It grows faster than almost any other tree in the jungle and because it floats so well, it's brilliant for making rafts.'

'And model airplanes,' added Marco wistfully.

'How do you know all this stuff, Beck?' asked Christina.

'My parents lived all over the world and my father was a survival expert,' replied Beck. 'He taught me everything he knew. When I was a kid, he showed me how to make shelters in the wilderness and find food and water. Sometimes it was in the jungle, sometimes in the desert or in the mountains. I made my first abseil down a cliff when I was five years old.' He sighed wistfully, but then turned his attention once more to the job in hand. 'There's no time to waste,' he told the twins. 'We must hurry if we're going to leave tonight.'

There was a note of urgency in his voice now. 'We need a sharp blade to cut this tree down. It shouldn't be too difficult as the wood is so soft but this trunk is more than half a metre thick. With the logs from three or four trees like this we should easily be able to make a raft that's big enough.'

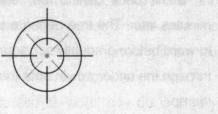

CHAPTER 13

As the boys went in search of more balsa trees, Christina hurried off in the direction of the hacienda. She reappeared a few minutes later, a leather sheath slung around her waist. Long tassels hung down almost to her feet. 'Dad's machete,' she said, pulling the steel of the blade free and turning it in her hand so that the sharpened edge flashed in the sunlight. 'He likes wearing it when he's on his own at home. Mum says it makes him feel like a conquistador.'

The team set to work. Aiming a series of heavy diagonal blows at each side of the trunk of the balsa tree, Beck sent chips of wood flying into the air. Marco picked a piece up and turned it over in his hand. It was as light as a feather and the colour of porridge oats.

'Stand back behind me,' shouted Beck a few minutes later. The tree began a slow-motion topple forward before gradually accelerating and smashing through the undergrowth onto the ground with a dull thump.

Repeating the process with the other trees they had found nearby, they lopped off the branches and cut each trunk into three until twelve logs lay side by side on the jungle floor like giant matchsticks. As the boys admired their handiwork, Christina went in search of some bamboo for the decking layer. Adrenalin surged through her veins as the blade of the machete swung through the air and dug into the base of a clump of tall bamboo poles with a loud *ker-chunk*.

She remembered the tales her father used to tell her of the tribe of women warriors who once lived in the forests of the Amazon just a few hundred kilometres away over the mountains. A glint of fierce determination sparkled in her eyes as, one by one, the giant bamboo stems fell free.

'All we need now is some long lengths of vine,' said Beck as they dragged the last of the bamboo poles back to the beach. 'Not exactly a problem round here.' He pointed out the best lengths for the purpose, and Christina and Marco took it in turns to hack away at the thick tendrils that clung to the trunks of the jungle trees.

With all the materials for the raft now assembled, Beck demonstrated how the vines should be woven between the balsa logs at both ends and across the middle of the raft, and then pulled together under tension. A top layer of bamboo, laid crosswise, strengthened the structure and formed a deck.

When they had finished, Beck went off into the undergrowth; he reappeared a few minutes later dragging more wood behind him.

'Mangrove,' he said. 'It's much harder than balsa but grows just as fast. We can make the mast out of this and lash bamboo across it in a frame for the sail. The Indians would have used palm leaves woven together, but I seem to remember sleeping in some cotton sheets last night.'

As Christina set off back to the hacienda to raid the linen cupboard, the boys lashed together the mast and the bamboo frame for the sail. Then they lowered the finished structure into place through the circular hole that Beck had cut in the deck. 'Perfect,' he said as they slotted it into place. 'Just enough movement to let it swivel. Now we'll be able to change direction when the wind gets up.'

When Christina returned with the sheets, Beck cut four lengths of vine about the thickness of his little finger and threaded them through the edges of the sheet like the stitching on a wicker basket. Once the sail was in place, he lashed more lengths of the mangrove together in the shape of a large A. When he had finished, he wedged it into the deck platform at the other end of the raft from the sail. 'One tiller,' he said, rubbing his hands together with the satisfaction of a job well done. 'All we need now is a long pole to use as a rudder.'

By now the sun was sinking in the sky and the shadows of the trees were growing longer by the minute. 'Just one more rather important thing,' said Beck as they looked at the raft in the gathering gloom. He swung the machete down hard into the green spongy skin of a large object like a giant football that lay under a nearby palm tree. As it split open, a milky sap oozed out.

Picking up the coconut and shaking it, he sent arcs of milk squirting over the deck of the raft before passing it on, first to Christina and then to Marco, so they could do the same.

'I name this ship the *Bella Señora*,' said Beck solemnly as they passed around the coconut, drinking a toast. 'Long life to all who sail in her.'

'To the *Bella Señora*,' echoed the twins.

CHAPTER 14

When the naming ceremony was over, Marco led the way back to the hacienda, where Beck disappeared upstairs and the twins began filling a large hamper, ransacking the kitchen for provisions. Marco had persuaded Señora Cordova to go home early, saying that they were too tired to eat much supper and would be going to bed early. She had left them some food out to make sandwiches.

As they were adding a few last afterthoughts, Beck reappeared. He was clutching a shiny black object with a large colour screen. 'Global Positioning System,' he explained. 'Otherwise known as a GPS. I take it with me everywhere I go with Uncle Al. He's forever getting lost so it comes in handy every time. It talks to satellites in space to pinpoint your position.

With this we'll know exactly where we are to within about two metres anywhere on Earth!'

The twins watched as Beck punched instructions into the keypad and the familiar outline of South America appeared on the screen. As he repeatedly punched a button marked ZOOM, Christina felt as if she were landing in an alien spaceship: the outline of Colombia drew ever closer, until at last they were hovering over the streets of Cartagena itself.

'This little gizmo tells you everything. High tide tonight is just after midnight, and once we're out at sea, the current should be running east. Exactly where we need to go. I've calculated it should take us less than two days to reach the shore where Gonzalo landed. We'll be able to find more food and water in the forest. But let's eat something now and then sleep for a few hours.'

The hacienda was quiet as the grave when Beck woke the twins, just before midnight. Out of his bedroom window he could see two police cars blocking the driveway beyond the electric gates, the tip of a lighted cigarette and the silhouettes of two policemen chatting idly together. A full moon hung in the sky like a ripe cheese.

The three ghostly figures made their way across the lawn and along the forest path to the beach, the twins carrying a hamper between them.

Beck fetched the machete from where it had lain hidden and slung the belt around his waist. The GPS was safely in his pocket, the map strapped around him under his shirt.

'We're in luck,' he whispered as the twins dragged the raft from its hiding place under a clump of palm trees near the water's edge. 'The breeze is strong and it's blowing offshore so it should be easy to get clear of the bay. But no more talking now until we're at sea.'

Working in silence and following the instructions Beck had given them earlier, the crew of the *Bella Señora* dragged the raft down a short strip of sand to where the waves were breaking on the beach. As they reached the water, Christina felt the hairs on the back of her neck stand on end: a dark shape was swooping out of the jungle towards her. She ducked as it swerved around her head and Ringo came to rest on top of the mast.

'Looks like we've got a stowaway already,' muttered Beck. 'Who said he could come anyway?'

'He's our mascot,' said Marco.

'Always best to have stocks of fresh meat for the larder, I suppose,' replied Beck, eyeing up Ringo, who put his head on one side and glared at Beck suspiciously.

As Christina climbed onto the raft, Beck and Marco swung the hamper into place beside the mast before Beck waded into the surf, dragging the raft behind him. Steadying it from the beach end, Marco followed behind. As Beck had warned, launching a raft from the beach at night was not going to be easy.

As he dragged the raft into the surf, the words of the famous Beaufort Scale came into his mind. He had learned it as a child on a sailing holiday in Cornwall with his dad. Invented by an admiral called Beaufort around the time of the Battle of Trafalgar in 1805, it helped sailors guess the strength of the wind from the telltale signs of the sea. Flat calm – 'sea like a mirror' – was force zero, while a hurricane

– 'air is filled with foam and spray' – was a force twelve.

Beck looked out to sea, where the wind was already blowing spume off the tops of the waves. '*Many white horses are formed. A chance of some spray,*' he chanted. A force five at least, he guessed.

The secret was to drag the raft to the point beyond where the waves were breaking – as far as they could before the water became too deep to stand in. By the time Beck was in a position to hold the raft steady, the water was already over his shoulders and he could taste the salt water in his throat.

The rip of the undertow sucked at his legs and he knew he would not be able to continue walking on the bottom for much longer. 'Now!' he bellowed as, flexing every muscle in their bodies, he and Marco dragged themselves onto the raft.

As Beck had instructed, Christina clung onto the tiller for all she was worth to keep the raft pointing out to sea. If a wave caught them side on now, all their efforts would be in vain and they would be swept back up onto the beach.

And then suddenly the rocking movement of the raft began to ease as the breeze caught the sail and they began moving smoothly out to sea. Within minutes the beach had disappeared into the inky blackness as a silver trail of moonlight stretched out across the Caribbean Sea.

'There's no way back now,' shouted Beck in triumph. 'Lost City, here we come!'

As if in mocking answer to his cry, the crew felt a shudder. The raft stopped dead in its tracks as the surf surged and fell beneath them. For an instant it seemed to hover in mid-air. Then a surge of water picked them up and threw the raft sideways, knocking the crew onto the deck.

'We've hit a reef!' screamed Marco. 'Hold on, hold on!'

Ringo cawed and circled overhead. Christina felt water under her feet as she clutched desperately at the tiller to avoid being swept overboard. Beck and Marco were clinging to the mast for dear life. And then, just inches from Beck's outstretched hand, the hamper began to slide slowly across the deck.

Slipping this way and then that as the raft

juddered against the reef, for a moment the hamper looked as if it might have wedged itself between two strips of bamboo. But as Marco made a final despairing lunge, a wave swept it into the foaming surf beyond the despairing clutch of his fingers.

And then suddenly it was all over. The deck was level once more and the shuddering ceased. Beck felt for the machete, still safely attached around his waist. The swell beneath them settled into a gentle undulating motion and the raft was sailing sweetly towards the open sea. Behind them they could see the froth of white water over the jagged peaks of the reef from which they had so narrowly escaped.

The *Bella Señora* was sailing safely once more.

But the hamper – and all its contents – was gone.

CHAPTER 15

The crew of the *Bella Señora* lay exhausted on the deck. Like a horse let loose from its stable, after a flurry of bucking and tossing its head, the raft was moving smoothly at last. The sail, stretched tight like a balloon, reminded Beck of the belly of one of Uncle Al's beer-drinking friends, and soon the stiff breeze had blown them beyond the headland of the bay.

Beck held the tiller while the twins sat on either side, holding the vines that controlled the sail. No one spoke. Even Ringo had stopped cawing and was perched, still as a statue, at the top of the mast. Only the *slap-slap, gurgle-gurgle* of the waves broke the silence. The loss of the hamper with all their provisions for two days at sea was a terrible blow.

It wasn't the lack of food that worried Beck. Humans, he knew, could survive for up to three weeks without eating. And there would be plenty of jungle food once they were back on land again. But the loss of the water container was serious. They would lose water from their bodies quickly in the hot sun, and drinking sea water would be fatal. Their kidneys would be poisoned by the salt and afterwards each little swallow would feel like their throats were being scraped with sandpaper.

But now was not the time to worry the twins. And besides, he had another confession to make. 'It's my fault,' he said at last. 'I should have checked that the hamper was properly lashed to the mast.' He winced and closed his eyes. 'And there's something else you should know.' The twins gazed questioningly back at him. 'The GPS slipped out of my pocket. I had it tied to my belt but the coral must have sliced through the string when we hit the reef.'

A brooding silence fell over the crew. Then Beck laughed. An ear-splitting guffaw that caused the startled Ringo to jump from his perch and fly in circles around the raft. He came to rest again on the edge of the deck, as far from Beck as he could get without landing in the sea.

'Come on, guys. Look on the bright side. Things can only get better,' Beck pleaded. 'Uncle Al says the first rule of survival is to keep smiling. If you're still alive, there's always hope. Once me and Dad survived for five days on a raft much smaller than this one. Dad was on a mission on the *Green Warrior* and we were attacked by pirates in the South China Sea. We had to live off rainwater and fish until we made it to land.'

'Yes, but how do we navigate without a GPS?' asked Christina, unable to disguise the catch of fear in her voice. Her question hung accusingly in the night air.

'With the stars and the moon,' replied Beck. 'The first sailors crossed huge oceans on rafts just like this one. And I'm pretty certain they didn't have a GPS.'

He pointed up into the inky darkness, where the stars sparkled like diamonds in the night sky. 'Each one of those little pinpricks of light is a sun just like ours,' he went on. 'But our ancestors didn't know that. What they saw were their gods striding about the sky. Men, horses, fishes – all the creatures of the jungle. Beats telly any day.'

'But how does that help us find our way to the Lost City?' asked Marco, unconvinced.

'According to Gonzalo's map, we need to keep sailing east from here. So as long as we know which way is north, it's easy,' Beck explained.

'But which way *is* north?' asked Christina, a note of exasperation in her voice. 'I can hardly tell which way is up or down. There's nothing but sea, sea and more sea out here. We're on a floating prison surrounded by nothing but water.'

'There's one star that never moves,' said Beck. 'It's like there's a huge maypole in the sky and the rest of the stars dance around it. And that one solitary star is always pointing north. And guess what?'

'What?' said Marco, sounding cross now.

'It's called the North Star, dumbo,' said Beck.

'Yes, but how do you know which one it is?' shot back Marco. They gazed up at the pinpricks of light that twinkled in the velvety darkness. 'There are millions of them. It's like trying to find a needle in a haystack.'

'More like a grain of salt in a sugar bowl,' said Christina. She took a deep lungful of the cool night air and sighed. 'Sometimes at home I just lie on my back on the lawn and stare up at the sky. It makes me feel so tiny. I wish we were . . .' Her voice tailed off.

'You've got to think of the night sky like a friend, not a like a bogeyman out to get you,' said Beck. 'But you have to get to know it first.' He pointed up into the darkness and traced a pattern across the sky with his outstretched finger. 'The Plough – Ursa Major – call it what you like. It's one of the easiest constellations in the sky to find. It looks like an old-fashioned plough.'

'Looks more like a saucepan to me,' said Christina. She paused and stared up at the heavens with her head on one side. 'But I see what you mean now. And I suppose "the Plough" does sound a bit more poetic than "the Saucepan".'

Now Beck was tracing a W in the sky not far to the left of the Plough. 'Cassiopeia,' he said before the twins could ask. 'Draw one imaginary line through the central point of the W and another between the two stars that make the outer edge of the saucepan. And that's it. Where the two lines meet is the North Star. If we sail towards that, we'll eventually arrive at the North Pole.'

'But we're trying to find the Lost City, not the North Pole,' said Marco.

'No problem,' Beck replied. 'We know the Sierra Nevada mountains are directly east of Cartagena so all we need to do is sail . . . thataway.' He pointed at right angles to the star. 'Which happens to be exactly the direction the current is taking us.'

For the second time that night, Christina had reason to be thankful for Beck's quiet reassurance and the panic in her stomach at last began to subside. It seemed incredible that this schoolboy Brit, only a few months older than the twins, had learned so much about nature and how to survive against all the odds. But her eyelids were beginning to droop now as the night drew on.

CHAPTER 16

Beck let the twins sleep as the *Bella Señora* sailed on into the night. Hours later, Christina woke with a start. Something slimy had brushed against her face and she let out a stifled cry. Whatever it was had tangled itself up in her hair. Flapping her arms and shaking her head wildly from side to side, she desperately tried to brush the creature free. But just when she thought it had gone, something else was moving against her legs. And then her arm. And then her face again. A torrent of slime was raining out of the sky.

And then, as suddenly as it had begun, everything was still. Christina peered nervously out through the gaps in her fingers, which were now clasped tightly around her face. It was already light and the sun, like a giant tangerine, was slowly rising above the horizon. There was a weak sound of slapping all around the deck.

This time it was Beck's turn to collapse in helpless laughter at the twins' discomfort. 'Sorry to wake you,' he said. 'I thought you might like room service for breakfast, but it arrived a bit sooner than I thought.'

Five flying fish lay on the deck, their mouths opening and closing as their wings flapped vainly in the silent spasms of their death throes. Marco made a grab for one as the creature made a last attempt to spread its wings and fly before falling lifeless to the deck.

'Hit them over the head with the machete handle,' shouted Beck, handing it over. 'It'll put them out of their misery.'

Marco floundered around the deck on his mission of mercy as Christina watched in silent horror. Finally all five fish lay still.

Beck calmly picked up the nearest one and drew the wings apart. 'Flying fish actually have four wings,' he explained, as if he were a teacher in a school biology lesson. He laid the fish in front of the twins. 'When they're chased, they accelerate through the water. Then, when they reach the surface, they spread their wings and just glide over the top of the waves. Neat way to escape, huh? Unless you end up landing on a passing raft, of course. Feeling hungry?'

Christina was looking at Beck in disbelief. 'You're not really suggesting we should eat these things, are you? Raw?'

'Not the guts, of course,' said Beck. 'Although we can always use those for bait or suncream.' He looked towards the horizon, shielding his eyes against the giant orb of the sun. 'And we're going to need some today by the looks of it.' Lining up the fish carcasses, he carefully removed the wings. 'I'm not sure what we can do with these, to be honest.'

'Maybe stitch them together and make our own wings,' said Christina. 'Then we could fly to the Lost City. It would be a bit quicker than this.'

Ignoring her, Beck picked up the machete and, with quick swipes of the blade, expertly removed the heads one by one. Then, after slicing the blade

101

through the soft white underbelly of each fish in turn, he pushed his finger inside the cavity so that the guts flopped onto the deck with a liquid squelching sound.

'Now that's what I call bait,' said Beck with a satisfied smile as he sifted through the gooey mass. 'And the oil from the livers is brilliant for sunscreen. We'll dry them in the sun and it'll be better than anything you can buy in the shops. It's full of vitamin D. That's what protects your skin against the sun. And it rubs on nicely. Smells a bit but great when it's do or die. Factor twenty at least, I reckon.'

'Yuck,' hissed Christina. 'That is really gross.' She wrinkled her nose with disgust at the line of little orange sacks that Beck was carefully lining up along the side of the deck.

'It's amazing how much less they seem to smell when you're really hungry and thirsty,' said Beck in a matter-of-fact voice. 'Anyway, I suggest we tuck in now before the sun gets too hot and the fish go manky. But before we eat, we need to get as much fluid inside us as we can. If we don't, we won't be able to digest the fish properly.'

Beck lay down on the deck and, taking hold of one of the flying fish in both hands, he squeezed. A dark liquid the colour of plum juice oozed out of the pinky-brown flesh and dripped over his lips. 'Tastes rather bitter,' he said nonchalantly when he had finished drinking. 'But it sure does cool your mouth down.'

Disgust and thirst battled it out on the twins' faces. This was a good lesson, thought Beck. His new friends would need to learn fast.

'OK, who's next? Chrissy, hold out your hands.' As if under a spell, Christina held out her cupped hands. Her stomach felt queasy and she was breathing heavily.

Beck gathered the fish heads into a pile before picking up the machete in one hand and one of the heads in the other. Then, with a deft turn of the blade's tip, he flicked an eye out of its socket and watched it drop into Christina's hands. The girl flinched but kept her hands locked out in front of her as Beck removed both eyes from all five of the fish heads.

Christina looked down. Ten glassy eyes stared

back at her. She could feel the contents of her stomach rising towards her throat and swallowed only just in time to stop the follow-through. Marco breathed deeply and turned his head away.

'No takers?' asked Beck. 'Well, guys, if you're not going to have yours, I certainly will. If we leave them any longer they'll start to ferment.'

Christina watched, frozen to the spot, as Beck took one of the eyes from her cupped hands. Then he threw back his head and, with the eye pinched firmly between his thumb and first finger, squeezed. A thin watery fluid dripped onto his tongue. Then he dropped the eye into his mouth and began to chew. One at a time he picked up two more eyes and repeated the process.

'That is absolutely disgusting,' said Marco, trying hard not to gag. 'You're very welcome to mine if you're still thirsty.'

'I wouldn't give up your share of anything, Marco. You can't be squeamish if you want to survive,' replied Beck. 'Wow, that feels better,' he said, wiping his sleeve over his mouth. He reached over to pick up another of the fish eyes from Christina's cupped hands. But this time Christina drew her hands away.

'Mine, I think,' she said. Her voice sounded fierce and determined. Transferring the eyes to her left hand, she used her right to pick up one of the jelly-like discs, then threw back her head. And squeezed. Keeping her eyes tight shut, she grimaced as a dribble of fluid slid slowly down the back of her throat. Then, keeping her mouth wide open, she dropped the shiny disc onto her tongue, lowered her head and, without opening her eyes, began to chew. Then she swallowed.

Beck watched her grimace as the slimy goo slithered down her throat.

'*Buen apetito!*' he said.

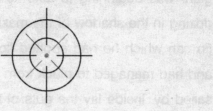

CHAPTER 17

Beck gazed listlessly down into the glassy stillness. It was late afternoon at the end of their first day at sea and the wind had dropped. The sail of the *Bella Señora* hung lifeless from the mast, looking ominously like a bed sheet once more.

After their five-star breakfast of raw fish washed down with eyeball fluid and blood, Beck had produced a little magic. A few teaspoons of dew had collected overnight in the folds at the bottom of the sail and the crew had gratefully dampened their lips and wiped away the taste of fish.

The fish livers had dried quickly in the sun and they had smeared their exposed skin with the thick droplets of oil that oozed to the surface. For a while the breeze had cooled their skin but the sun's brutal glare was beginning to take its toll. The twins lay dozing in the shadow of the mast. Marco cradled a tin can which he had spotted floating in the water and had managed to pluck from the waves as they sailed by. Inside lay the guts of the flying fish in a putrefying mass.

Beck smiled. Marco was learning fast. Gone now was the disgust of just a few hours before. Anything that could help them survive was precious. Including the fish guts. But Beck's throat felt parched and hunger was beginning to gnaw at his stomach. The water looked so pure and cool and tempting. He let his hand dangle for a while in the silky stillness, longing to feel its coolness on his lips.

But somewhere deep inside, alarm bells were ringing. That way only madness lay. Throughout history shipwrecked sailors had been unable to resist the temptation to drink sea water and had quickly gone insane.

A grisly thought sprang into Beck's mind. He remembered the day Uncle Al had taken him to the Louvre, the famous art gallery in Paris. The *Mona Lisa*, with its crowds of jostling tourists, had not interested him. Instead he sat for nearly an hour, staring at a huge canvas that covered almost the entire wall of one of the gallery's other rooms.

It was a painting called *The Wreck of the Medusa* by the artist Géricault. Uncle Al told him the real-life story. A French ship had been wrecked in a storm and some of the crew had escaped on a raft. After several weeks at sea the crew had become so desperate and hungry, they began to eat each other.

He looked over to where Christina lay curled up, her leg stretched invitingly towards him. Beck raised his eyes to the heavens and laughed out loud. 'I must not eat Christina's leg,' he chanted. And then repeated it three times, as if he were back at school, writing out lines in detention for Mrs Armington. 'But parrots are just fine,' he added, suddenly jumping to his feet and making a mock charge at Ringo, who hopped around the deck, screeching loudly and flapping his wings in alarm.

The commotion shook the twins out of their stupor. Marco groaned and crawled towards the side of the raft, saying he was about to throw up. Grabbing his arm so his palm was facing upwards,

Beck pressed his thumb hard into the veins in the centre of Marco's wrist. Marco's shoulders slumped and he felt the muscles in the pit of his stomach relax. The desire to vomit slowly lifted.

'How did you do that, Beck?' asked Marco, amazed.

'It's an old acupuncture technique my mum taught me,' said Beck. 'It's best not to be sick if you can possibly help it. You'll lose so much body fluid, and you know what that means.'

'More eyeballs,' said Christina. 'Yum, yum!' She yawned and shook her head, her earrings flashing in the bright sunlight. She looked up to see Beck staring intently at her.

'I think I've got it,' he said.

'Aye, aye, skip,' said Marco, who was now feeling better and was looking at Beck curiously. 'But we haven't!'

'Your earrings, Christina. Give me your earrings.'

Christina spun her head out of the way as Beck made a grab for her ears. 'What are you doing?' shouted Marco. 'You've been drinking the sea water, haven't you?' A short scuffle broke out as Marco leaped to protect his sister, the strength in the boy's skinny frame taking Beck by surprise.

'Fish hooks, loco,' hissed Beck. 'Your sister is wearing a pair of fish hooks in her ears. We need food. But she doesn't need to look pretty. And if you do that again, you'll capsize the raft.'

Marco loosened his grip and Beck wondered whether the boy realized how easily he could have tossed him aside. But Marco was showing signs of stress and now was not the time for Beck to show off his skills as a junior judo champion.

As Christina reached for the lobes of her ears, Beck could see tears welling up inher eyes. 'I'm sorry,' he said quietly. 'But we need food. Unless we eat some fish, the fish will soon be eating us.'

Dropping her head to first one side and then the other, she removed the earrings with deft flicks of her wrist. 'I'm beginning to hate you, *Inglés*,' she said. 'Mum gave me these as a present after she came back from a trip to Brazil.' She dropped them into Beck's outstretched palm. 'And I expect them back with a fish supper attached.'

Beck sat down with his back to the mast as

Marco took over the tiller. The wind was beginning to get up again and the sun was dropping lower in the sky as evening drew on. Working away at the soft metal with the blade of the machete, he had soon fashioned a pair of fish hooks. He held them up for the twins to inspect.

'All very clever, skip,' said Marco. 'But we don't have any fishing tackle.'

'That's where you're wrong,' said Beck, untying the laces of his trainers.

But Christina wasn't listening. She was jumping up and down, pointing at the water in front of the raft. 'Look! Look! Over there!'

Beck peered down into the depths. Dark shapes were zigzagging at high speed around the raft. Like fleeting shadows, they moved so fast that they were gone as quickly as he could focus on them. Christina let out a cry of delight as one broke through the surface, arching into the air ahead of them. It was followed by another and then another, until they were surrounded by leaping creatures like acrobats at a circus.

'Dolphins,' laughed Marco as arcs of water

droplets from their smooth white underbellies sparkled in the evening sun. The twins had seen dolphins in aquariums, jumping through hoops as a trainer threw fish into their mouths. But this was the first time they had encountered them at sea.

Their spirits soared as the dolphins soared and spun in an intricate dance. Christina gasped again as a mother with two babies pirouetted through the air, turning somersaults before plunging back into the water.

'*Bailamos, bailamos*. Let's dance, let's dance,' she shouted, doing a little jig across the deck.

'This beats synchronized swimming any day.' Marco's eyes were alight. 'They're just so graceful.'

'Look, look. She's smiling at us,' Christina said in delight as the mother dolphin leaped through the air once again. And then suddenly, like the sun disappearing behind clouds, they were gone. Christina crumpled to the deck, not knowing whether to laugh or cry.

'Why did they have to go so quickly?' she cried as Marco put his arm around her and they slumped in a deflated heap against the mast.

But Beck wasn't listening. He was staring out to sea, his eyes making a slow sweep of the water around them. Sensing that something was seriously wrong, the twins sat bolt upright, following Beck's gaze.

And then Marco saw it. It felt like a knife had been plunged into the pit of his stomach. A sinister black triangle like the sail of a miniature pirate ship was slicing through the water around the boat.

No one spoke. There was no need.

The *Bella Señora* was being circled by a shark.

CHAPTER 18

The twins watched, mesmerized. The black fin was slicing through the surface of the water like the blade of a knife through cling-film. With idle flicks of its huge tail, it cruised ominously just below the surface of the water; the evil silkiness was so different from the arching playfulness of the dolphins just a few minutes before.

But Beck's gaze had shifted. No wonder the shark had shown up. A river of red goo was dribbling over the side of the raft. During the encounter with the dolphins, the tin can with the fish guts had been knocked over. Talk about a red rag to a bull, thought Beck. More like a tin of tuna to a starving cat.

His mind raced. He knew only too well what a

shark could do to a raft like the *Bella Señora*. Memories of his father flashed through his mind. They had been fishing on Australia's Great Barrier Reef, taking time out from a Green Force mission. Throwing Beck a knowing look, his father had poured blood from a bucket of fish guts into the sea. Within minutes, three tiger sharks were circling the boat.

Beck had learned some sobering facts about shark behaviour that day. Lesson One: tiger sharks can smell a single drop of blood in an Olympic-sized swimming pool. Lesson Two: they can swim at speeds of up to forty miles an hour. Beck had worked it out. That was faster than he could manage flat out downhill on a racing bike.

Grabbing the can, he turned it upright and wedged it against the mast before shovelling in as much of the bloody slop as he could before it slipped back out through his fingers. 'Probably best if the rest of the family don't join the party,' he said, wiping the slime from his hand on his shirt. 'Those fish guts make great bait, but a tiger shark wasn't quite what I had in mind. But we've got to keep still.

The more we move around, the more excited that shark's going to get. If we're lucky, it might lose interest and leave us alone.'

But the shark was showing no signs of losing interest. The telltale trail of blood had clearly come from this fragile pile of sticks above him and he had an empty stomach that needed filling. Christina clutched at Marco in terror. The fin was charging straight towards the raft. The creature's wedge-shaped snout had flipped over on one side and for an instant she was staring straight into its glassy eye.

Beck winced in relief as, at the last moment, the shark dived under the raft before reappearing again on the far side. Like a guard circling the perimeter of a prison camp, it continued its patrol, every now and then making sudden, unexpected darts towards them. By now the twins' faces were fixed in horror. With their arms wrapped around the mast in a vice-like grip, they were mumbling something Beck could not hear. Christina dropped her head and made the sign of the cross.

The impact, when it came, took the crew of the

Bella Señora completely by surprise. The deck flexed, lifting them high into the air as the shark's nose smashed into the balsa logs beneath. In a blind panic, they rolled towards opposite sides of the raft while the mast shuddered and shook. Ringo was nowhere to be seen.

Grabbing at the mast to steady himself, Beck leaped to his feet. 'That was just a mock charge. If he charges us again, he'll sink the raft. Chrissy, Marco – we've only got one chance.' Even Beck was struggling to stay calm.

The shark was coming round again now, but this time it had tightened its circle and was no more than seven or eight metres away. 'Untie one of the vines from the sail.' Beck's eyes were fixed like search-lights on the fin, tracking its every move. 'It doesn't matter which one. Just untie it. Now.' His voice was taut with urgency.

Rigid with fear, Marco and Christina worked in tandem like zombies. Their eyes stared straight ahead of them, unable to take in what was happen-ing. With trembling fingers, they dragged the vine from where they had so carefully threaded it through the sheet and around the bamboo frame of the mast when they built the raft.

Marco cursed. 'Why did we tie this so tightly? It just won't come free.'

Beck was holding the tiller with one hand as he stood on the edge of the raft, watching the ever-decreasing circuit of the shark's fin through the waves. 'Quick, guys. Quick, quick.' His voice was quieter and calmer now. He knew the twins were doing everything they could as fast as was humanly possible.

'Done it!' shouted Marco at last, sweat pouring from his face.

Beck had removed the machete from its sheath and was holding it in his hand, mouthing encouragement to himself as if he were preparing for a race. A look of calm determination spread over his face. He knew for certain that he only had one chance and he was not about to blow it now.

As Marco fed him the vine, Beck looped one end through the metal ring that dangled from the handle of the machete. As his fingers danced around one another, he mouthed the famous scouts' mantra: '*Up through the hole. Round the tree. Back down the hole*.' He could tie the sailor's famous bowline knot in his sleep, but never before had he needed it like he needed it now.

Pulling the knot tight, Beck glanced at the shark again. 'Tie the other end to the mast,' he hissed through clenched teeth. 'Clove hitch is best. But anything, anything will do so long as it holds. If we lose the machete, we're done for.'

Then the shark charged. Like a torpedo, it was coming straight for the raft. Christina screamed as Beck threw himself across the deck. Rows of jagged razor teeth were now clearly visible above the surface of the water. To the twins on the far side of the raft, Beck looked as if he were about to be swallowed whole by the shark's jaws, its teeth framing the outline of his body like a trophy on a game hunter's wall.

For an instant Beck stood rooted to the spot. His right arm held the machete high over one shoulder as every muscle in his body flexed beneath his skin. Then, with a sudden flick, he sent the blade of the machete circling through the air like a boomerang whistling towards its prey.

To Marco, the scene unfolded like the slo-mo replay of a winning shot in the final moments of a World Cup final. The flashing steel of the blade spun through the air with a *whop, whop, whop* sound before slicing through the creature's head and eye. A livid red line opened up along the side of its head and a jet of blood spurted high in the air.

Then the shark's snout crashed down into the water, just missing the side of the raft. The impact sent a wave pounding over the deck, catapulting the far side of the raft into the air. For the third time in as many minutes, the crew clung to the mast for their lives.

As the shark's head came to rest near the side of the raft, it looked for a moment as if it were smiling at them in surprise. The flow of blood was soon a gushing torrent and the water around the raft turned scarlet. Its tail flapping wildly, the creature shuddered as the life force drained out of it like air from a burst tyre. At last the snout dropped slowly below the surface of the waves and the carcass slumped onto its side, the jaws hanging limply open.

With a determined grimace, Beck plunged the machete further into the creature's brain. Unable to believe the danger was finally over, Marco and Christina still clung to the mast. Beck punched the air in triumph. His face and arms spattered in blood, he sank down onto the deck as the creature floated lifeless beside the raft.

For a few moments no one spoke. The sail flapped loosely in the breeze. Then, without warning, Beck sat bolt upright, muttering to himself as if in trance. 'Cut it free. Cut it free. If we don't cut it free now, every other shark in the sea will be around us like flies.'

Pulling himself back onto his feet, Beck tugged at the handle of the machete, desperately trying to free it from where it was buried deep in the side of the shark's head. But try as he might, he was unable to pull it out. Marco let go of the mast, and together the two boys tugged at the handle with all their might.

Then, with one final heave and a sickening

sucking noise like a boot coming free from a bog, the blade finally came loose and the boys staggered back across the deck, dripping with blood. Christina grabbed the tiller as the shark and the raft slowly drifted apart.

The battle for the *Bella Señora* was over.

CHAPTER 19

Beck let the raft drift. Bruised and exhausted after their battle with the shark, the crew slept as the *Bella Señora* sailed on into the night. In what seemed like the blink of an eye, the sun slipped around the Earth and was rising once more in front of them. The colour of the sea began to change. From black, it changed to purple. From purple to red, and from red to pink.

Beck was calculating their position. The wind and the current were taking the raft at a steady pace towards the rising sun. 'Sun rises east, so we sail east,' muttered the exhausted skipper, as if trying to convince himself of what his brain was telling him. They had been at sea now for two nights and a day. At an average of four or five knots per hour,

Beck estimated they must have sailed around 150 miles.

Flocks of birds were visible in the far distance and cumulus clouds were popping into the sky like blobs of cotton wool. Beck peered up at them, deep in thought. A tinge of green stained the flat white base of the clouds. 'Reflection from the jungle,' he said at last. 'And those birds are pelicans. Which means we can't be far from—'

'Land!' shouted Marco, jumping to his feet and pointing excitedly. Christina was awake in an instant, shaking the sleep from her tired limbs and peering into the haze in the direction in which Marco was pointing. The outline of the highest mountain peaks could just be seen on the horizon, patches of snow glistening in the morning sun. A smile broke over Marco's face. 'The famous Sierra Nevada mountains of Colombia. Lost City, here we come!'

But Beck was already looking back out to sea, an expression of concern on his face. Clouds like banks of layered snow were massing on the horizon. 'Bad news, guys. Looks like nimbostratus clouds. We could be in for a bad storm later in the day. Our only hope is to reach land before it breaks.'

Beck was grappling under his shirt. A buckle dropped down as he dragged a plastic map case onto his lap. 'I bet Gonzalo could have done with one of these,' he said, spreading it out on the deck. Inside was the conquistador's map. 'Never leave home without a waterproof map case. That's my motto.'

'It looks more like the map of a rabbit warren than a map of a Lost City,' said Christina as the twins peered over Beck's shoulder at the intricate mosaic of lines scrawled in faded, black ink.

'I've been thinking about it again,' said Beck. 'I think it's in three parts. Three different sections of the journey.' He looked up at the mountains, where the jagged outline of the highest peaks was etched against the deep blue of the morning sky.

Suddenly, with a shout, Marco grabbed the map case from Beck's grasp and held it up to the sky. A thick wavy line had been drawn across the top of the parchment. Lines ran off it down the page, with here and there a cross and some words in an ancient Spanish script. Marco held it up to his eyes so that the light shone through the parchment. He squinted at it, moving it slowly from side to side. Finally he held it still.

'Look,' he said, the excitement rising in his voice. 'This must have been Gonzalo's view of the mountains when the ships landed. He's got every little ravine and peak. The outline of the mountains is almost exactly the same as the line on the map. You can see it through the parchment. They're an almost perfect match.'

Under a notch in the high mountains, a straggling line led down to a large cross. Next to it, in bold capitals, were the words:

AQUI. 8 DIC. AÑO DE. NUESTRO SEÑOR MDXXII

'Here. December the eighth. The Year of Our Lord fifteen twenty-one,' whispered Marco. 'This must be where the conquistadors landed. It fits completely. The lines running down from the mountains must be rivers. The other lines must be paths through the jungle. It's all beginning to make sense.'

Euphoria gripped the crew as land drew closer. But as the sun passed overhead and the afternoon wore on, the wind began to blow more strongly. Brooding storm clouds were massing above them. Almost black towards their base, they were stacked hundreds of metres into the sky. At its top, one of the clouds had flattened out like an anvil in a blacksmith's forge.

'Q nims,' said Beck. 'Cumulonimbus clouds. Bad sign. I was hoping we would have landed before the storm broke but no such luck. We could do with some fresh water but that little lot could drown a city.'

Christina was grim faced. 'I don't need a survival expert to tell me that, Beck. Those clouds look like they could sink the *Titanic*, not just the *Bella Señora*.'

The breeze was now blowing fiercely towards the land. The sea was surging beneath them, lifting the raft and dropping it again in the troughs between the waves. Beck could see strips of white sand where the beach was sandwiched between the green of the jungle and the blue of the sea. All along

129

its length, the line was broken by the dark gashes of rocky headlands.

He gazed anxiously up at the sky. If the storm had come just a few hours later, they could have chosen their landing spot at leisure. But with the strength of the wind and the current, steering with the tiller was becoming almost impossible. As the shore came closer, Beck winced. His worst fears were being realized. The raft was being blown straight towards a headland between two bays. Stretching out towards them was the telltale white froth of a line of surf where a sandbank had built up beyond the headland, and the waves split in two like the traffic on a motorway intersection.

Further in, on either side of the headland, giant rollers thundered onto the beaches. 'It won't be long now,' shouted Beck above the roar of the wind. 'I'll do what I can to keep the raft in the hollows between the waves. If we start surfing on the crests, we'll be thrown straight onto the rocks.'

As Beck shouted instructions, Christina and Marco did what they could to steady the raft. Ringo had abandoned his perch on the mast, his screeches blown away on the wind as he circled above them. But now a huge wave was raising them up and the twins felt themselves being lifted skywards, as if a giant hand were hurling them towards the sandbank.

When it came, the impact shook the raft with a terrifying shudder. A corner had hit the sea bed, and as the next wave picked them up once more, the raft spun round, flinging the twins into the raging surf. For a split second Beck could see them flailing desperately in the tossing waves and he heard a squawk from Ringo, far above. Then he lost sight of them as another huge wave crashed over the deck, throwing him against the mast. His legs felt like jelly as he fought desperately to cling on against the suck of the undertow.

But the water was getting deeper again now and the waves more regular. The raft had been lifted off the sandbank and was hurtling towards the beach. As the mountain of water around Beck grew taller, the back of the raft was being sucked upwards by a following wave.

Realizing the danger at the last moment, Beck threw himself clear as the wave hurled the raft up the beach. Pitched forward in the seething foam, he felt his body smash against the hard sand before the drag of the undertow locked around his legs and began pulling him out to sea once more. In a fleeting moment he could see Marco being tossed around in the surf before a second wave came crashing down, pummelling him into the sand. Breaking free of the waves, he gasped for air and struggled to stand as the suck of the surf dragged his legs from under him.

Marco was beside him, tumbling over and over like a rag doll in the merciless surf. Throwing out a hand, Beck grabbed the boy's shirt just as another huge wave lifted them up and threw them up the beach. And now at last they were free of the waves as they staggered forward and collapsed exhausted on the sand.

'We've done it! We're alive!' Beck was picking up handfuls of sodden sand in relief. But a look of horror had crossed Marco's face. His cheeks were ashen and his eyes staring.

'Christina . . .' he whispered quietly. 'Christina.' His voice rose to a crescendo as he jumped to his feet and began racing along the beach, scanning the waves. 'Christina!' he screamed. 'Christina!'

Beck was behind him now, his eyes desperately scanning the line of the beach and the raging surf in front of them.

But the third member of the crew of the *Bella Señora* was nowhere to be seen.

Christina was gone.

CHAPTER 20

Beck shook the sleep from his exhausted body. He'd collapsed under a palm tree, his limbs leaden and bruised. Not far off, he could hear Marco groaning and turning restlessly. After a fruitless hunt for Christina, their shouts drowned out by the roar of the surf, the boys had reluctantly abandoned the search until first light.

After they landed, Marco had been hysterical, running blindly back and forth along the beach, screaming Christina's name. Realizing the danger of sapping their remaining energy, Beck had eventually calmed the boy down and convinced him that Christina had probably been washed ashore further up the coast. 'We're still alive, so there's no reason why she won't be,' he had reasoned, trying desperately to keep Marco's spirits up. He wished Ringo were around, but there had been no sign of the parakeet since the raft had started to pitch in the surf. At least they still had the machete, safe in its sheath around his waist.

Now the sun was rising over the headland into a deep blue sky. The tattered remnants of the previous night's storm clouds were strung out along the horizon like rags on a washing line. Scattered along the white sand of the beach lay the wreckage of the *Bella Señora*. The broken mast and the balsa logs rolled listlessly in the waves. The sail, battered and torn, had been tossed onto the beach like a sodden rag.

Beck shook his head. Something was flashing across his closed eyelids like a doctor's bright torch. He tossed his head irritably, as if flicking hair out of his eyes, and groaned. The beginnings of a headache for sure. One that would get far worse as the sun rose higher in the sky. He swallowed. He could already feel the dryness in his throat and the day had hardly begun.

But then the flash came again. And again.

Shielding his eyes with his hand, he peered out across the beach towards the headland, where it stuck out from the bay like a crooked finger. Something very odd was happening. Marco was awake and skipping down the beach, dodging from side to side as if playing a game of touch rugby. The beam of light was dancing over his body as he chased it along the beach towards the headland.

But now the beam was still again and had settled into a pattern. The flashes came in bursts of three: short, long, and then short again. Beck recognized it at once. Morse code. SOS. The international distress signal. The lost crew member of the *Bella Señora* was signalling to them from the cliff on the headland.

'I just did as you told me, Beck,' said Christina when the three teenagers were reunited later that morning. Marco was beside himself with joy and Christina wiped tears of relief from her eyes. 'All I remember was a huge wave picking me up and dragging me into the sea. I didn't fight it but just went with the current. I must have been dragged into the next bay.

Then, suddenly, there was sand under my feet and I was thrown up onto the beach.

'I couldn't see the raft anywhere and I just prayed you'd been taken into the other bay,' Christina went on. 'When it got light, I climbed out along the headland and saw the wreck of the raft, and I guessed you must be nearby. Then I remembered my mirror. I'd forgotten I had it on me. I keep it in a little vanity bag in my trouser pocket for real emergencies like parties. I couldn't believe my luck when I found it was still in one piece.'

By now, the sea was flat and calm. In the shallows of the bay it had turned the colour of lime juice, a few gentle ripples throwing shadows on the sandy floor like clouds on a summer's day. 'It looks just like one of Mum's holiday brochures,' Christina commented. 'But somehow I don't feel like I'm on holiday. Paradise isn't really paradise when you've just been shipwrecked.' She looked around, and then asked, 'Hey, where's Ringo? Have you seen him? Surely he must have reached land OK?'

The others shook their heads and Beck tried to reassure her that the parakeet would turn up soon.

The reality of their situation began to dawn on him. 'We need to get sorted fast,' he told the twins. 'Otherwise we'll end up fried and starved and we can forget about seeing Uncle Al and your dad ever again.'

Christina pointed back along the headland towards where the jungle started to climb towards the mountains. Massive boulders, smooth and circular like giant cannonballs, had tumbled down from the cliffs onto the beach, as if a race of giants had been playing marbles along the seashore. 'There are some caves up there, left behind by the boulders,' she said. 'I slept in one earlier.'

'Perfect,' replied Beck. 'If we make camp in one of those, it should keep us warm and dry tonight, especially if it rains again. It'll save having to build a shelter until we get further into the jungle. But we need to make a fire and find some water. There'll be no shortage of seafood round here.' He pointed towards the rocks further along the headland. 'After all, we never got a chance to use these . . .'

Beck felt in the pocket of his trousers and drew out a small, soggy piece of rag, a tiny remnant of what had once been the proud sail of the *Bella Señora*. He opened it carefully and held up a couple of objects that dangled from his fingers like a pair of upside-down question marks. The sharpened points of Christina's earrings glinted in the sunlight.

'But first we need to get some water inside us. Fast.' He ran his hand over the wrinkled grey bark of a tree that arched up through the undergrowth towards the sky like the trunk of an elephant.

'Coconuts,' he said. 'God's gift to the shipwrecked sailor. They're stuffed full of good stuff – vitamins and minerals and all that. You just have to be careful to drink from the unripe ones. If you drink too much from the ripe ones, they'll give you the runs and you'll end up more dehydrated than you started. But it's OK to eat the meat from both.'

Clasping the tree in his cupped hands, Beck wrapped his legs around the trunk so that his thighs were gripping it like a monkey. Then, in short, sharp movements, he hauled himself up with his hands, the trunk held in a vice-like grip between his legs.

'I learned this trick from a sloth monkey in Borneo,' he shouted down to the twins. 'They move a bit slower but it's a great way to climb a tree. Tough on the family jewels though.'

Marco sniggered and shot a sideways glance at his sister. Christina raised her eyes to the heavens and pretended she hadn't heard.

'Mind out below.' Five huge coconuts thudded onto the ground next to the twins as Beck quickly slithered back down to join them. He hacked through the tough husk of one with the blade of the machete. After quenching their thirst with the cool milk, they cut open another and then another before munching on the soft milky flesh inside, which Beck had already chopped into bite-sized chunks.

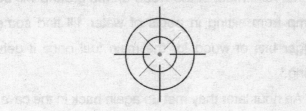

CHAPTER 21

The afternoon was drawing on by the time they went in search of shelter for the night. As Christina had promised, a series of holes like shallow caves had been left high in the cliffs where boulders had dropped down onto the beach.

'We need to build a fire,' said Beck. 'But first we need some tinder and kindling to get it going. Chrissy, can you find some tinder? Ferns, grasses, even dried-out fungus, that sort of thing. It's got to be paper-dry so you can scrunch it up in your hand. Look in the cracks between the branches.'

He turned to Marco. 'Marco, you find some kindling. Sticks or small branches that can be broken up. Look for dead branches that aren't on the ground but hanging in the trees if you can. After all that rain, most of the wood on the ground will be damp from sitting in pools of water. I'll find some bigger bits of wood for the main fuel once it gets going.'

An hour later they met up again back in the cave. Along with some dead grasses, Christina was crushing a dried-out bracket of fungus she had broken off from the base of a palm tree. Beck set to work preparing the fire just outside the entrance to the cave.

'We're in luck. This would have been a whole lot harder yesterday during the storm.' He cleared away the debris and made a circle with some nearby rocks. Then he set out the tinder, kindling and fuel in neat piles so that everything was within easy reach.

'I think you've forgotten something,' said Christina as Beck stood back to admire his handiwork. 'We don't have any matches.'

'No, but I do have this.' He fished out a bootlace that was hanging around his neck and held up two metallic objects. Christina examined them curiously. One was a short metal rod; the other looked a bit like a blunt razor blade.

'Fire steel,' said Beck. 'I carry it everywhere. It's made of magnesium mixed in with other stuff. When you strike the rod with the scraper, it sends off showers of sparks and – hey presto – with a bit of practice, fire! Matches are useless when they're soaking wet anyway. And this'll last ages.'

He stood over the tinder of dried grass, which he had fluffed up into the size of a tennis ball. Then, with a small stick, he poked a hole into the centre. Striking the metal scraper against the rod with deft flicks of his wrist, he sent a shower of sparks raining down into the centre of the tinder.

Then, with a *whumph*, a lick of flame burst into life, followed by a loud crackle as the grass began to burn fiercely. Next Beck built a tepee of small twigs over the grass from the kindling Marco had collected. Within moments it was ablaze and the twins started to pile on thicker and thicker sticks.

'Be careful now,' warned Beck. 'Fire is fragile. It needs air to breathe. If you smother it, we'll have to start all over again. Just take it easy and we'll be there in no time.' As the twins backed away, Beck blew long, steady puffs of air into the base of the fire. The flames began to leap up through the pyramid of sticks.

Broad smiles burst onto the twins' faces as the heat warmed their bones. 'Perfect,' said Beck. 'I feel a seafood and coconut stew coming on. Any takers?'

The twins went in search of more wood to feed the flames while Beck climbed down onto the rocky headland, filling his pockets with limpets as he went. The trick was to dislodge them with a sudden kick before they sensed danger and clamped down like superglue onto the rocks. Then, moving slowly and quietly, he scanned the rock pools, watching for the telltale darts of crabs and stranded fish.

The sun was already setting when, an hour later, he headed back to the cave. Marco and Christina were grinning like Cheshire cats as they sat contentedly feeding wood onto the fire, which was already sitting on an impressive bed of glowing charcoal. The flickering flames of the campfire threw eerie shadows onto the back wall of the cave.

Beck smiled proudly as he held up his prize catch. His fingers were clasped tightly around the brown shell of a huge crab, the pincers flailing harmlessly in the air. Holding it out towards the twins so they could get a better look, he made a sudden dart with the crab towards Christina.

'*No, inglés!* Get away from me, English boy!' she screamed as Marco collapsed in laughter. 'For that you can go without your water ration.'

Beck looked down at the fire, where steam was rising from the tin can that he had last seen filled with fish guts aboard the *Bella Señora*.

'Found it thrown up on the beach,' said Marco proudly. 'And guess what?'

Beck raised his eyebrows enquiringly. 'You found Uncle Al and your dad at a beach bar drinking cocktails?'

'That's not funny, Beck,' said Christina. 'I bet they won't be having a crab supper tonight, wherever they are.'

Beck realized at once he had upset the girl and looked at her and said sorry.

Christina remained silent. Then, without warning, a smile broke over her face. 'What I was going to say is that I found about three pints of rainwater in the trunk of a rotten tree. And we managed to scoop it out with the tin.'

'Top girl,' said Beck approvingly. He turned away and smiled to himself. Survival was as much to do with what went on inside their heads and hearts as it was to do with their struggle against the elements. Keeping focused and keeping smiling were the first steps. Beck knew he had a battle on his hands to keep their morale high and their eyes on the prize of finding their father and Uncle Al.

He soon had the dark, rubbery flesh of the limpets sizzling on a hot stone, then he lowered the crab into the boiling water; its pincers flailed wildly in the air before finally sinking into the depths of the tin can. After their ordeal at sea, their first proper meal in more than two days seemed like the best food any of them had ever tasted. As the stars came up and the fire began to burn lower, the twins slumped together against the back wall of the shallow cave. Beck lay awake thinking and planning, before he too was overcome by sleep.

He woke with a start. The fire was almost out now

and a chill was creeping up his back. Sitting up, he stared down along the line of the beach as his eyes slowly adjusted to the darkness. All seemed quiet and yet he could sense in his bones that something was wrong. Then he heard a sound: the gentle pad of footsteps on the sandy surface of the cliff, where it gently descended to the beach.

His heart thumped in his chest and his eyes scanned quickly from left to right. Both the twins were still sleeping soundly beside him. Beck slowly stood up. Hardly daring to breathe, he walked silently in the direction the sound of the footsteps had come from. As he rounded the corner of the cave, he stopped and listened once more. Only the faraway thunder of the waves crashing onto the beach broke the silence.

Then he looked down. In the moonlight he could see the distinctive outline of footsteps leading away from the cave. Taking care not to make a sound, he followed the prints back along the headland and down towards the beach, where the dense under-growth of the forest met the sand.

The eerie glow of fireflies shone back at him out

of the inky darkness. Suddenly, without warning, his eyes came to rest on two shiny discs, which reflected back at him the bright silver light of the moon. In an instant he was back once more among the party-goers in the carnival crowd outside the Hotel Casa Blanca in Cartagena.

Beck was gazing straight into the eyes of the Indian.

CHAPTER 22

'You saw what?' asked Marco as the boys huddled around the fire early next morning. Beck had coaxed the flames back to life, blowing gently on the embers until the remnants of unburned wood caught alight once more. As they picked over the remains of the previous night's meal, an unappetizing broth of watered-down coconut milk bubbled gently in the tin can.

Beck was still lost in thought as he relived the events of the previous night. The instant he had seen the eyes of the Kogi Indian, he had instinctively thrown himself into the cover of some bushes. But when he peered back into the jungle, all signs of the man had gone. His pulse racing, Beck had returned to the cave. He had stared restlessly up at the stars while the twins slept. There was no point in waking them: tracking the Indian before the sun came up was pointless and they all needed rest.

'I suppose you think I dreamed it again,' said Beck. 'Like in the crowd at the carnival. Well, I didn't then and I didn't last night. And this time I've got the evidence to prove it.'

'Beck wasn't dreaming,' said Christina, who had disappeared along the headland towards the beach and had now rejoined the boys. 'I followed the tracks and found where Beck's footprints stopped and the others led off into the jungle. Somebody was watching us last night. And not just in Beck's dreams.'

A morning mist still hung in the air as Beck led the twins back to the spot where he had hidden from the Indian. 'This is where he was standing when I saw him,' he said a few minutes later after a brief search in the jungle. 'You can tell from the outline of the prints. They're deeper and more blurred than the ones before and after.'

Beck recalled the time he had spent with the San Bushmen of the Kalahari Desert in southern Africa. His father had been living among them on a special assignment with Green Force and the San had taught Beck the secrets of tracking animals in the wild. It was they who had taught him to read the world under his feet like an open book.

Following the prints where they led away into the jungle, Beck suddenly stopped dead in his tracks. Without warning, the footprints had changed direction and were heading straight back to the beach. Beck shuddered. All the time he had been scanning the forest from his hiding place under the bush, the Indian must have been watching him from behind.

'Maybe there's a reason for all this,' he said, gazing along the gentle curve of the palm trees where the footsteps disappeared around the bay. 'If Gonzalo landed on this beach, as the map says, this is where he would have met the Kogi Indians. And they must still know where the Lost City is. Either way, it's time we found out.'

Beck led the way along the edge of the beach, where the tracks soon faded away in the soft sand. After about an hour they reached the far side of the bay. Looking back, they could barely make out the outline of the cave where they had spent the night on the headland in the far distance.

The palm trees thinned out as the sand merged into the long grass surrounding the low-lying marshy land of a mangrove swamp. They heard the sound of pelicans' wings whirring overhead. Footprints were now clearly visible on a path that led away from the sea into the mountains. From the jumble of prints in the soft clay, Beck could tell at once that the path was in regular use.

In the distance, smudges of smoke stained the bright green of the jungle where it rose up into the mountains, and Beck could see the dark outline of a circle of thatched roofs. Following the path through the long grass, they emerged on the edge of the mangrove swamp; a raised path led towards the village. Suddenly a familiar screech came from the grove of jungle trees surrounding the huts.

'Ringo!' cried Christina as they crouched down in the cover of the long grass. 'It's Ringo. I'd recognize that screech anywhere. Thank goodness he's OK.'

'Wait here,' said Beck. 'It's better if one of us goes ahead. If I'm not back in an hour, go back to the cave and wait for me there. We need to know if the Kogi Indians are friend or foe.' As the twins looked on nervously, he made his way along the path, listening intently at each bend for the sound of footsteps coming towards him.

As he approached the village, he could at last make out the formation of the huts. Three rings of huts had been built around a clearing with larger huts with more elaborate roofs at either end. As he reached a grove of trees outside the village, Beck crouched down in the undergrowth and peered towards a gap in the ring of huts where the path disappeared into the village. Ringo was nowhere to be seen.

Wisps of smoke still curled above the huts, but not a sound came from the clearing within. All Beck could hear now was the thumping of his heart. Stepping out from the protection of the trees, he clutched at the handle of the machete where it hung from his waist and strode boldly down the short avenue between the huts.

CHAPTER 23

A smell of cooking hung in the still air and logs smouldered on campfires with pots dangling above them. A leather sandal lay on the ground outside one of the huts next to a plate made of palm leaves. But no human sound broke the silence.

Beck circled slowly around on his heels, the hairs on the back of his neck standing on end. The sun was high in the sky now, making him squint as he peered nervously into the murky darkness of one of the huts. Suddenly he let out a muffled cry and stepped back into the clearing, his heart thumping against his ribs. Like stars in the night sky, four pairs of eyes stared back at him.

Then Beck heard a movement behind and spun round. In front of him was the Indian from that fateful night in the carnival crowd in Cartagena. Those familiar piercing eyes were now just a couple of metres away and staring directly into his own. Beck swallowed hard and opened his mouth to speak. But the words would not come. His mouth felt parched. The Indian did not move.

'I have come . . . to . . . to . . . find . . .' Beck stammered at last, hardly able to get the words out. He started again. 'My friends and I were wrecked on the beach near here and we have no food or water. We mean no harm.'

Realizing he was still clutching the handle of his machete, Beck laid it down slowly on the ground before raising his palm in a sign of peace. The Indian did not move but continued to gaze straight into Beck's eyes.

Under the hot sun, Beck was beginning to feel light-headed. Part of him wanted to run. To run now, and to run hard. But his legs felt like lead. Then the Indian began to speak. Not a single muscle on his face was moving and his lips were quite still. But his words echoed deep inside Beck's head.

'My name is Kojek,' said the voice. 'I am an elder

of the Kogi Indians. This is our home. Without our welcome, you are an intruder here.'

Beck opened his mouth and tried to speak. But again not a single word came out.

'Come,' said Kojek. 'The Younger Brother must learn something of our ways.'

By now a small crowd of villagers had emerged from their huts around the clearing. They stood in family groups, the children in front of the parents, as if they had been expecting a visitor and had turned out in their Sunday best. Jet-black hair framed the high cheekbones of their brown faces. But their features did not move. Not a smile or a frown. Neither welcome nor reproach.

From a larger hut at the far end of the clearing, a small group of men now appeared. They too wore the white tunics of the Kogi tribe, with hats that tapered to a point like the roofs of their huts. Kojek led the way towards the group of elders, who parted to let them through, then led the way into the hut.

After the bright sunlight, the world went black as Beck followed him in. By the time his eyes had adapted to the darkness, he found himself sitting cross-legged in the centre. The hut was divided into four sections, with a fire in the middle of each tended by one of the holy men of the Kogi tribe.

'Younger Brother,' Kojek said. 'We welcome you to our home. We, the Kogi people, are the Elder Brother. We are the guardians of the Earth. Our work is to protect the mountains among which we live.'

Kojek paused for a while before continuing. 'The first time other Younger Brothers came here, you killed our people and burned our homes. Your leader found our holy city in the jungle and took away the life blood of the Mother. Soon after, we deserted the city. When the Younger Brother returned again, he could not find the city and took a terrible revenge.'

Beck's head was spinning.

Kojek was speaking once more. 'Because of the deeds of the Younger Brother, our world is dying. Our sacred city has lain covered by the jungle for many centuries. To you it is a lost city but for us it is a city that sleeps. A treasure was stolen from us. You must give back to the Mother what your ancestors stole. Only a Younger Brother can return it to the place from whence it was taken.'

Kojek was standing again now, his arms outstretched to Beck.

'Younger Brother, the treasure which you call gold is the blood of the Mother. Without her life blood, the Mother will die. On our mountain peaks, the eternal snows are melting. Soon the rivers will dry up and the people will die. The Elder Brother cannot heal the world for much longer if the Younger Brother continues to let her bleed.'

Beck was staring deep into Kojek's eyes. Nothing seemed real any more. The village, the hut, the Kogis – everything seemed to be dissolving into thin air. He felt his hand groping under his shirt for the golden amulet. Since they had first discovered it in Gonzalo's secret hiding place, the toad had hung around Beck's neck like a good-luck charm.

He held it tight in his hands and felt a wave of tiredness wash over him.

Then all around him went black.

CHAPTER 24

Beck could see himself standing on the beach, staring out to sea. The hut, the Kogis, Kojek – all were gone. And something inside him had changed too. Yes, it was still him all right. Still Beck Granger standing here thinking his own thoughts. But he had entered a different world – he was dreaming that the Kogis were going to show him their past.

His eyes scanned the horizon nervously. Just a few hundred metres out to sea, beyond where the surf was breaking, was a sight Beck had never witnessed before outside the pages of a history book. Two Spanish galleons were anchored in the bay, their pennants fluttering in the breeze.

For a moment he stared at them in disbelief, unable to move a muscle; unable to quite believe what he was seeing. But something else had caught his eye now: rowing boats were being lowered into the water from the decks of the ships and Beck could hear the gruff shouts of the crew over the sound of the waves. The men in the boats were shouting up to those on the ships as chain gangs loaded supplies over the rails. Meanwhile, pairs of oars were emerging from the sides of the rowing boats as they bobbed up and down in the swell.

And now another more precious cargo was being lowered slowly and carefully down to the men in the boats. The objects were long and thin, and before each one was handed down, powder from a leather pouch was poured into one end before being rammed home with a long stick. With a shock of recognition, Beck realized what they must be.

Turning their prows towards the beach, the rowing boats were soon coming fast towards him. Near the back of the first boat, Beck could see a man, who was clearly the commander of the boat, shouting orders. Sitting calmly while the men around him rowed, he fixed his eyes on the mountains beyond the beach.

164

Spread over his knees was a parchment and he was moving his head from side to side, scanning the land ahead of him. As the boats came closer, Beck was able to make out the man's features in more detail. He reeled back in shock. The profile of that long, straight nose was unmistakable.

Then Beck heard a shout. The men at the front of the lead boat were pointing in his direction. And they did not look friendly. A glint of Spanish steel flashed in the sunlight and the oarsmen redoubled their efforts as the boats changed direction and headed straight towards him.

Beck felt his legs sprinting up the beach, along the path through the mangrove swamp towards the village. The men of the village were huddling together now. Women and children were gathering in the village clearing and Beck could hear the scared crying of the children as they clung to their mothers' legs.

The men were clutching spears and had spread out across the path beyond the entrance to the village.

And then Beck saw what his heart most dreaded.

The commander himself was advancing along the path towards him. The man's beard was more ragged than in his portrait and the eyes more cruel. But Beck knew for sure now who he was looking at.

His legs felt weak as he tried to rise from his crouching position in the undergrowth. He could see every detail now, every slight change of expression, on the man's face. Behind him, the men from the rowing boats were strung out in a line, scanning the horizon nervously from right to left. And then, as the arc of the man's gaze crossed his own, Beck froze. There was no doubting it now. He was staring into the eyes of the twins' ancestor, the famous conquistador, Don Gonzalo de Castillo.

For a moment no one moved. Beck's ears were burning and he could hear every sound in minute detail. The sailors were breathing heavily and he could hear the chink of chain on metal. Behind him, in the forest, the call of a hummingbird sounded like a song from an opera. In front of him, a tiny bird with bright yellow feathers and a hooked beak was flitting among the white flowers of the mangrove swamp.

Gonzalo raised his arm, his palm facing towards

Beck as if giving a sign of peace. In response, the men of the village slowly began to stand, the points of their spears facing towards the sky and no longer towards Gonzalo and his men. Suddenly there was a flash, followed by a bang and a puff of smoke.

At once the sounds of the jungle fell away, drowned out by the noise of screaming and shouting and musket shots. Then he felt an agonizing pain in his left shoulder like the blow from a hammer; his body crumpled and he dropped to his knees.

All around him was chaos. Musket muzzles flashed every few seconds as Gonzalo's men disappeared behind clouds of smoke. And now somebody was dragging him back along the path towards the village. His shoulder had gone numb and he could feel blood seeping through his fingers as he tried to cover the wound with his hand. He was among the palm trees near the entrance to the village when the arms that were pulling him suddenly went slack and a Kogi man fell down beside him. His eyes were closed and his head hung limp, slumped on his chest.

Beck's head swam, and for a while he lost track

of what was going on around him. When he came to, Gonzalo's men were running past him into the village. Flames were leaping from the thatched roofs of the huts and acrid smoke was billowing into the sky.

And now Beck was being pulled along the ground once more. But this time it was Gonzalo's men who were dragging him, shouting and cursing. His shoulder felt like it was being stabbed repeatedly with a knife; then he was thrown roughly to the ground in the centre of the clearing. He watched helplessly as Gonzalo strode into the burning village and one of his men pointed towards where Beck was lying.

Gonzalo was standing over him now, staring down into his face. Beck could see every detail of the conquistador's features. The painting in the ballroom of the Casa Blanca, the statue in the square and the portrait at the hacienda had caught the likeness well. But there was something they had all missed. The nobility of the features had gone; cruelty curled on Gonzalo's lips and glinted in his eyes.

Now he was kneeling down beside Beck, clutching something in his fist. As he lifted his arm, a gold chain flashed in the sunlight. The familiar features of the toad amulet, its eyes bulging, its stomach bloated, its mouth gaping, stared back at him.

For a moment Gonzalo dangled it in front of Beck's face. Then he knelt closer and whispered in his ear.

'*Perdido no más*,' he said.

CHAPTER 25

Beck had been tossing and turning in his sleep. But now, the muffled chanting of the Kogis had soothed his troubled dreams and the slow, rhythmic beat of a drum calmed the *thump, thump, thump* of his racing heart.

Beyond his closed eyelids, he could dimly see the light of morning and smell the freshness in the cool air. The raucous crowing of a cock broke through the quiet and he realized that a voice he recognized was calling his name. For a few delicious moments Beck thought he was back home again on Uncle Al's farm in the country. Aunt Kathy was calling him down to breakfast and he could smell frying bacon and freshly baked bread.

But now someone was shaking him and gently

slapping his cheek and he sat up with a start. '*Buenos días*, Señor Granger,' said the voice. 'Sleep well?' It was Christina.

Beck wiped the sleep from his eyes and looked around. Sunlight was pouring through the entrance of the hut. But everything had changed since the previous evening. The Kogis had gone and he and Christina were alone. In a pot hung over a fire, something that looked like thin porridge was bubbling gently.

Christina handed him a bowl full of the steaming gruel. 'Tasty,' she said, raising her eyebrows to the heavens. 'Not!'

'But probably the best meal we're going to have in a long while,' replied Beck. 'So we'd better make the most of it. Where's Marco?'

'He's talking to the villagers,' said Christina, nodding her head towards the door. 'The Kogi found us yesterday after you disappeared. We waited and waited, and then a group of villagers appeared out of nowhere and brought us here.'

She smiled timidly, as if unsure whether to go on. 'It was as if they knew we were there. They told us everything, Beck. About how the Kogi are the Elder Brother and we are the Younger Brother. And the story of Gonzalo stealing the toad amulet from the Lost City. And how his men burned down the village in revenge when they couldn't find it again.'

Beck nodded. 'They told me too.' He paused and took a deep breath. 'And some!' He told Christina about the dream and his vision of Don Gonzalo and his men burning down the village. When he had finished, he took the toad amulet from around his neck and held it up to the light.

'And this is what caused all the trouble. Kojek, the Indian I saw in the square that day in Cartagena, says it's their offering to the Earth Mother that was held sacred by his ancestors. Gonzalo stole it and now it must be returned.'

'Do the Kogis know that Dad and your uncle were kidnapped, Beck, and why we need to find the Lost City so urgently?' asked Christina, trying hard to remain calm. 'I'm so worried.'

'I don't know,' replied Beck. 'But we musn't lead them into any more danger. We have to go on by ourselves if we want to rescue Uncle Al and your dad.'

He stood up and walked over to the doorway of the hut. Outside, groups of Kogis were going about their daily chores. Marco was talking to some villagers but when he saw Beck, Marco broke off his conversation and headed towards the hut.

'Sleep well, *amigo*?' He beamed, grasping his friend in a welcoming bear hug.

A small group of inquisitive children had soon surrounded the boys, begging them to join in a game that reminded Beck of hopscotch. Christina was dragged in to assist but none of them was a match for the Kogi children. Afterwards they retreated to a corner of the village and sat down with their backs against a tree.

'The villagers are very friendly, Beck,' said Marco, 'but they want us to leave at once. They say the Lost City is in danger. I think they know about the gang and the kidnap.'

'If Gonzalo's treasure is not returned,' said Beck, holding up the amulet, 'they believe the mountains and the jungle will die. But before that we've got to find Uncle Al and your dad.'

Suddenly they heard a noise behind them. Kojek had silently walked up behind them and was standing watching. Once more the holy man's eyes bored into Beck's and he felt as if he were being slowly hypnotized. There was a sternness in Kojek's face and an urgency in his eyes he had not seen before.

Kojek took Beck's hand and led him across the clearing towards the entrance to the village. A group of young men were gathered around a fire; one of them was giving a young boy a tattoo. Nearby a young girl was having her long black hair washed by a group of older women. Marco waved to the group sitting cross-legged around the woman at the loom and, smiling, they waved back.

'I've been making friends,' said Marco as he held up one of the striped woven shoulder bags in which the Kogi carried their few possessions. 'It's a gift from the villagers. Could come in useful, you never know.'

A familiar screech greeted them as Kojek, the boys and Christina made their way out of the village and Ringo dive-bombed them from his perch on top of the Kogis' hut. 'Come on, Ringo!' shouted Marco. 'We're moving out. Time to go.'

As Kojek guided them along the pathway away from the village, Beck gazed pensively out over the mangrove swamp towards the sea. All was peaceful now and there was no sign of Gonzalo's galleons that he had seen in his dreams. In the far distance he could see the thin pale ribbon of the beach and the white stripes of waves breaking gently on the shore. Above them, palm trees reached towards the sky like giant feather dusters.

No one spoke as they followed in single file along a wide path that led through the jungle. Soon they began to climb steeply towards the mountains and the ghostly figure of Kojek disappeared into the distance in front of them. The bustling warmth of the village soon felt like a distant memory. The salty tang of the sea air had gone and a smell of damp, steaming earth hung about their nostrils as the suffocating heat closed in around them.

CHAPTER 26

No one could agree on when they finally lost sight of Kojek. But just as they finally realized he had gone, the path began to level out and they emerged from the forest on a hillside that looked back over the village, now hundreds of metres below. Terraced fields lay on either side of them.

'Maize,' said Beck in astonishment, looking up at the rows of stalks that towered above them. 'The Kogi must grow their crops up here because it's drier and sunnier. That's what we had for breakfast. The Indians grind up the corn into a paste – though I reckon it's much tastier as plain corn on the cob.'

Marco was carrying the machete now and, with deft swipes of the blade, lopped six of the tight green envelopes from their stalks and dropped them into the bag.

'Kojek must have led us here on purpose,' said Christina. 'It's like a final gift before he said good-bye.'

'And now it's up to us,' said Beck grimly. 'Kojek told me that the Lost City is only two days' walk from here but it will be tough going – the paths haven't been used for years. There's a river on a plateau east of here that leads to the city. And it's our only chance of finding Uncle Al and your dad.'

'*Through the valley on the plateau the river flows,*' said Marco, as if chanting a mantra. 'Kojek told me to remember those words too, Beck.' He paused and looked at his friend with knowing eyes. 'Or maybe I dreamed that.'

Beck smiled. 'We must trust the Kogis. Without a compass, there's only one way to navigate in a jungle, and that's to find a river. But you usually do that when you're trying to find your way *out*, not *in*.'

Beck looked into the distance. 'Once we get high up on the plateau though, we'll be able to see over the tops of the trees and find the river valley. Then we can follow it up into the mountains to the Lost City.'

'But what are we going to do when we find the Lost City?' asked Christina. 'What chance do we have against the kidnappers? Surely they've got guns.' She shuddered.

Beck took a deep breath. 'If we can survive being attacked by a shark, we can survive anything. *Keep hope alive*. First rule of survival, Chrissy. And you know what?'

The twins shook their heads.

Beck took the amulet from around his neck and dangled it in the sunlight. 'If we can survive the jungle and return this to the Lost City, I'm sure the Kogis will help us. Something tells me that they are going to be watching us – even from afar.' He paused. 'And if not, remember we also have the element of surprise.' There was a cry from a branch somewhere above them. 'Oh, and Ringo, of course,' he added, raising his eyes to the heavens.

As the day grew hotter, sweat began to pour off them. Christina's face had gone bright red and her mouth was hanging open as her head drooped.

'You're getting badly dehydrated, Chrissy,' said Beck. 'You need a drink. And you need it now.' He was staring up into the surrounding trees but the only sign of water Christina could see was the sweat dripping from her sodden clothes.

'Tarzan got it all wrong,' said Beck, pulling hard at a thick jungle vine clinging to the trunk of a tree. He took the machete from Marco and, holding it up as high as he could reach, carefully made a deep cut into the tough flesh of the vine. Then he slashed hard at the root, where it disappeared into the earth, before pulling up the severed end so that it hung over Christina's open mouth. Huge drops of clear water dripped onto her parched lips.

'Vines are more useful for drinking from than for swinging through the trees,' said Beck. 'Feeling better?'

Christina was wiping her mouth with the back of her hand. 'That's the nicest water I've ever, ever tasted,' she confirmed happily.

Beck cut another vine for Marco and a further one for himself. 'It's like sucking water into a pipette in a science lab at school,' he explained. 'The vines suck up water from the ground through the roots to feed the growing end. When you make the cut at the top, the water can't be sucked up any further. Then you cut it off at the root and gravity takes over. Hey presto, a hose full of water.'

The twins continued to drink greedily as Beck strode off into the undergrowth and returned with three long sticks. He gave one to each of the twins and kept one for himself. 'The only way to move quickly in the jungle is to slow down,' he told them. 'If you try to fight it, it just fights back harder. And it will rip your skin off your back unless you take it easy. Move like a dancer, not like a bull in a china shop. Drop your shoulders, swivel your hips.'

He picked up one of the sticks and went on into the undergrowth, moving the stick from side to side in front of him just above ground level. 'Keep watching for snakes. Move slowly and put your feet down hard. Snakes feel vibrations, so you want to give them plenty of warning. They'll only attack if they're cornered – most of the time, that is!' Beck grinned.

The path had all but disappeared now and a

dense tangle of foliage began to hem them in on all sides, pulling and catching on their clothes and skin. 'If you get lost in this stuff, you're in trouble,' said Beck, slashing at the thorns and tendrils that stabbed at them from every side. 'It's secondary jungle. The worst sort. The trees have been chopped down in the past, and when the light gets in, the undergrowth just goes crazy. It ends up strangling everything in the process. Including us.'

But something else had caught their attention now. Leap-frogging through the jungle trees above them, Ringo had been announcing his presence at regular intervals. Now, suddenly, his cries became more shrill than ever. 'That bird sounds more like a chainsaw than a parakeet,' muttered Beck under his breath.

In front of them lay a large, splintered branch. Ringo had come to a halt above it, and was flapping his wings and screeching wildly. 'You'd think the stupid parrot had never seen a tree before,' said Marco. 'I think it must have been blown down during the storm.'

Beck strode forward and was about to pull the

branch out of their path when he felt something inside him telling him to stop. He scanned the branch in front of him.

Suddenly his body froze. Beads of sweat rolled down his brow and he could feel the sting of salt in his eyes.

He was looking into the cold, unblinking eyes of a viper.

CHAPTER 27

The twins didn't have time to move a muscle. Like a Samurai's sword, the blade of the machete sliced through the air and, with a heavy thud, the sharpened steel struck home. Beck crouched over his prey, his body taut as an archer's bow. Then he relaxed and let out a long, low sigh. 'Shoousshh,' he said quietly. 'That was far too close for comfort. Thank you, Señor Ringo.' He blew a kiss skywards.

Beck dragged himself to his feet and turned to face the twins. The body of a giant snake hung twitching in front of them, impaled on the point of the machete. Beck ran his finger down the pinky-brown flesh. 'How about that for camouflage?' He raised his eyebrows in approval. 'Bushmaster,' he said. 'You

185

can tell from the zigzag shapes on its back. They're like black diamonds strapped round its body.'

He paused and gazed down at the dead creature in admiration. 'Biggest viper species in the world. And one of the most deadly too. Check out the length of those fangs. And its head is a triangle. Usually a sure sign in snake land that it's one deadly dude.'

He pulled the machete out of the bushmaster, before bringing it down hard again to sever the head. The body fell to the ground and he picked it up on the point of the machete. Meanwhile the head still lay on the branch in a pool of oozing, dark red blood. Its mouth gaped open in a ghastly smile and its eyes were fixed in a glassy stare. Its upper lip was still twitching and had curled back, revealing two huge fangs like the curved incisors of a sabre-toothed tiger. A thick trail of poisonous goo dripped onto the smooth bark beneath.

'Haemotoxin,' said Beck. 'If that stuff gets into your bloodstream, it will turn your blood into black pudding, along with the rest of you. All the poison's in the sacs under its head. The nerves go on working even after the head's been chopped off. It could probably still bite even now.'

He let out a sudden hiss and made a lunge at Christina, who yelped and jumped out of the way. 'I'll get you for that, *inglés*,' she said, a hint of steel flashing in her dark eyes.

Beck laughed and held the blade of the machete proudly above his head. The body of the snake hung limp in front of them like an eel on a fishmonger's hook.

'Pure protein,' he said. 'Just what we all need. We'll cook it tonight. If it weren't so deadly, we could have just taken it prisoner and killed it later. Keeps 'em fresher if they're still alive. Still, we've got meat and veg for supper now and it's not even lunch time.'

Beck edged towards Christina. 'And in the meantime it should make rather a fetching scarf.'

But this time Christina was ready for him. Quick as a flash, she grabbed the tail of the snake and wrapped it around Beck's neck. 'Suits you, *inglés*. Very smart.' She chuckled triumphantly.

* * *

Now that the tension had eased, they began to move more quickly. Taking it in turns to hack a path through the undergrowth with the machete, they walked in single file as they climbed ever higher. Warblers and hummingbirds flitted through the trees, bright splashes of colour against the endless canvas of jungle green. After a while the undergrowth became less dense and the trees much larger. Huge buttress roots fanned out from the base of their trunks like the webbed claws of a dinosaur.

'Primary forest at last,' said Beck, leaning on his stick and wiping his cheek with the back of his hand. 'This stuff will be easier to walk through. The trees have never been cut down so there's been very little light in here for centuries. No light and the undergrowth is better behaved. Even so, we'll be lucky to cover more than three kilometres in a day as the crow flies.'

'Pity we're not crows,' said Christina wryly.

'Or parrots,' said Marco, watching Ringo enviously as he glided serenely through the air above them.

They had reached a ridge high up on the edge of

the plateau now

dense thicket of b

as an elephant's

flecked with splas

their tops curled in

cathedral and shaft

sunlight through sta

The long day wa

there was an urgency .... At last,'

he said. 'Just what we needed. Bamboo's the best
material in the jungle for building a shelter. But we
must work quickly. It'll be dark in a couple of hours
and by then it will be too late. And if it rains tonight,
we're going to get soaked.'

Without warning, Beck plunged the point of the
machete into a bamboo stalk next to his head. As
the twins watched in amazement, water gushed out
and they drank eagerly. 'No need to go thirsty in the
jungle,' said Beck. 'If there's no rain falling out of the
sky, you can always be sure nature's stored it somewhere else.

'This looks like a good place for a camp,' said
Christina when their thirst had at last been satisfied.

, said Beck, turning in a slow
ing the surrounding jungle. 'But
eceive.' He picked up his stick and
earing the dead matter from the jungle floor
he had exposed the earth beneath. 'Look
there!'

CHAPTER 28

Beneath a seething mass of black they could just make out the soft green flesh of something that looked like a cross between a cockroach and a grasshopper. Every so often a limb would break free and twitch feebly before being swamped again by a sea of miniature black legs. Columns of reinforcements stretched out across the jungle floor in every direction. The twins flinched in disgust.

'Bullet ants,' said Beck. 'Get stung by one of those and you'll know all about it. It's like being burned with a red-hot poker. And if you've got the whole nest crawling over you, you're in big trouble. As that poor bug has just discovered. Ants don't do detours. If there's anything in the way, they just march straight over it. And if they're hungry, they'll just munch through it. And that includes us.'

Beck led the way out of the bamboo grove onto the edge of the ridge. He looked around and chose an area of ground that shelved away slightly. 'This is better,' he said after clearing away the undergrowth with his stick.

'There's only one rule when you build a shelter in the jungle. And it's exactly what Uncle Al says about buying a house.' Beck put on a posh English accent. '*Location, young man. Location, location, location*.'

The twins laughed as they remembered the eccentric Englishman in the panama hat. 'Wonder what he's doing now,' said Marco thoughtfully.

Beck pretended he hadn't heard. He wanted to keep their spirits up, not allow them to dwell on their worries. 'We're high up here,' he continued, 'so if it rains during the night, the water won't run down the hill and swamp our camp. These jungles aren't called *rain*forests for nothing.'

He gazed up into the tangle of leaves and branches above. 'And there's nothing up there to fall out of the tree and kill us. Most people who die in the jungle are killed by things falling on their heads. Rotten branches and coconuts are the worst. Not the most dignified way to go.'

He looked around, closely studying the jungle floor. 'And there are no animal tracks around either. Most of the big beasties hunt at night and follow the same paths. Especially if they lead to water. And if your bed happens to be in the way, they're not going to worry too much about trying to dodge round you.'

'Looks perfect, skip,' said Marco. 'What next?'

'A-frame bed,' said Beck. 'The principle is to sleep off the ground. That's where all the damp ends up and the creepy crawlies live. Just lash pieces of bamboo together in an A shape for the bed ends. Then you get two more poles and strap them to the frames halfway down. Looks a bit like a stretcher. Bingo! One bed.'

'But what do we lie on?' asked Christina.

'We can weave some vines and palm leaves across the stretcher bit to make a platform,' said Beck. 'Same principle for the roof of the shelter. It's like a screen woven across a frame of bamboos. If you want to get really fancy, you can cut some bamboos in half for guttering so that it channels the water away.'

While Beck cut down the bamboo, Marco went in search of tinder and wood for the fire and Christina cleared the ground for the camp with her stick. When Beck returned, he was brandishing some long strands of bark he had cut from a nearby tree. 'Stringy bark,' he explained. 'Works perfectly for cord to lash everything together.'

There was a shrill cry from above and they saw that Ringo was still with them, watching their activities with interest.

By the time the camp was finished, the daylight was almost gone. The flames from the fire were throwing eerie shadows into the surrounding forest. Marco was sitting on his pole bed, smiling proudly. Suddenly he let out a muffled curse and started to scratch hard at the back of his leg through his trousers.

'Don't scratch, Marco. Not like that. You'll break the skin and the wound will be full of pus by morning. Keep still now.' Beck had grabbed a branch from the fire and was blowing on the end. Kneeling

194

next to Marco, he rolled up the boy's trouser bottoms and held the glowing tip as close to Marco's leg as he could without burning him. Marco flinched as, one by one, five ticks dropped off his skin.

'Jungle basics,' said Beck. 'Look after your skin. It's not usually the big beasties that get you, it's the creepy crawlies.' He threw the burning branch back on the fire. 'OK, time for our feast.'

As the twins lay exhausted on their beds, Beck picked up the carcass of the bushmaster; earlier he had impaled it on a sharpened stick and stored it well clear of the jungle floor.

Grabbing the end of the severed neck, he began to peel the skin away from its body as casually as if he were taking off a jumper, and then slit the stomach of the snake. With a slurping noise, the guts slid out onto the ground. Christina looked away, trying to stop herself gagging as Beck picked them up and threw them into the flames. 'Don't want to attract uninvited guests,' he said, staring out into the surrounding darkness.

Silence fell as the meat gradually roasted over the flames. Beck had jammed the snake's tail into a splice before wrapping the rest of the body around the stick like a ribbon around a maypole. After a while the flames leaped higher and the fire began to sizzle and spit as the fat from the snake slowly oozed onto the embers below.

Lazily stretching out an arm from his sleeping platform, Beck turned the stick so that the meat cooked evenly. Finally he judged it was ready and cut it into steaks. They devoured it ravenously, washing it down with the water Beck had collected earlier in some makeshift mugs cut from sections of bamboo.

The meat and the warmth from the fire soon began to work their magic. Unable to keep their eyes open any longer, the twins fell into a deep sleep. For a while Beck fought the heaviness of his eyes and, taking Gonzalo's map out of the case strapped around his body, studied it once more in the light of the flames.

CHAPTER 29

Beck woke to the sound of thunder. A long throaty rumble like the roar of waves breaking on a beach. It was followed by the drumming of rain on the leaves of the jungle canopy far above. Soon a curtain of water was running off the lattice of palm leaves above his head. He flinched as an icy droplet exploded on his neck and began to run down his back. Beck groaned. Walking through the jungle in the heat and humidity was one thing. In the rain it would be a nightmare.

He peered out from under the cover of the shelter. Steam was rising from the campfire and the bed of glowing embers was hissing fiercely in the torrential rain. He was on his feet in an instant. Fire was precious in the jungle and the downpour had caught him off guard. Later in the day, even with the sparks from the steel, it would be almost impossible to light a fire because of the damp.

Just outside the camp was a tree with bark like the thick, fibrous skin of a coconut. Slicing through it with the point of the machete blade, he marked out a rectangle and roughly pulled it free. The fire parcel was an old trick the aborigines had taught him during his time in the Australian outback. As long as there was a steady supply of air, the charcoal from an old fire would smoulder all day. He pulled a red-hot stick out of the bed of embers and wrapped it in the thick envelope of bark.

By now the twins were beginning to stir. 'One moment I'm so hot I can hardly breathe and now I'm freezing again,' said Marco. 'This is nasty.'

They waited in the shelter of the camp until the worst of the rain had eased. Beck's mind was racing. If they could just find the river, the Lost City would finally be within striking distance and they would at last have a chance of rescuing Uncle Al and Mayor Rafael. From Gonzalo's map he could see that the river valley rose steeply to a second plateau high above them in the shadow of the mountain peaks. Here, he was certain, lay their goal.

Despite the rain, Beck urged them to get moving and to press on towards their goal. A moody silence fell over the twins as they followed Beck along the line of the ridge.

They had been moving for less than an hour when Marco pointed to a nearby tree. Ragged claw marks had been gouged deep into its trunk and thick globules of sap dribbled down the bark.

'Lucky it didn't use one of us as a scratching post,' said Beck.

'And lucky too that jaguars rest up during the day and hunt at night. So with any luck, our friend who made these little scratches will be having a siesta right now.' He paused and gazed into the depths of the surrounding jungle. 'Jaguars stick around places where they can drink. These tracks should lead to the river.' Beck pointed along the line of the ridge. Just a couple of metres away, the route the jaguar had taken was clearly visible, snaking away into the undergrowth.

Christina looked at Beck, terrified. Beck smiled.

'Jaguars go for weak prey – and you, Christina, are strong.'

As they followed the track deeper into the jungle, Beck's heart beat faster in his chest. He had decided not to tell the twins that the jaguar was a deadly threat. Bloodthirsty tribes like the Aztecs and the Maya had once worshipped the animal like a god. The jaws of a jaguar were so strong they could crush the shell of a turtle with one bite. They were also ferocious hunters. In the shadows of the rainforest, its trademark spots would be almost invisible. Until it was too late. Ambush was a fun game to play with your school friends. But not with a jaguar.

They had been following the tracks for about an hour when Beck put his finger to his lips. The twins stood rooted to the spot, the whites of their eyes standing out in the gloom. The cries of the jungle had become more familiar, and already they could recognize individual birds from their calls in amongst Ringo's squawks. But there was a different sound now. A long deep rumble like the sound of a double bass in the depths of an orchestra.

Minutes later, they were standing on the banks of

a wide, fast-flowing river. The rain had completely stopped and bright shafts of sunlight broke through the trees. Christina gasped in astonishment. Huge butterflies with spotted blue wings were fluttering over the dappled surface of the water and a bird with bright yellow feathers and a long curved beak was drinking at the river's edge.

But Beck wasn't looking at the river. He was standing as still as a statue, staring at the ground. A deep pawprint was clearly visible in the soft earth. Four circular pads wereset in a semicircle around a larger fifth. 'The mighty jaguar. The king of the jungle,' he muttered in awe. 'This must be the exact place he drank from just last night. But look, the tracks disappear into the water.'

CHAPTER 30

Christina gazed out in disbelief over the turbulent waters of the river. 'Do the tracks mean he crossed here? Surely he would have been swept away.'

'Jaguars aren't just ordinary pussycats, Chrissy,' said Beck. 'Jaguars *like* water. Dad told me once that he saw a jaguar swimming up a river dragging a deer in its mouth.'

'But look, Beck. The tracks reappear again further up,' said Marco, pointing along the riverbank.

Beck was silent for a moment, trying to understand what it meant. Suddenly it dawned on him. 'When the jaguar was here last night, the water level was lower. It must have walked along the bank. But the water's risen since and covered up its tracks. Now the level's rising even faster after all that rain.'

He knelt down to take a closer look at the map in its waterproof case. 'According to Gonzalo, the Lost City is on the far side of the river. And if we don't cross now, we may never get another chance. Further up the mountain, the river will be like a tsunami.' Already a telltale foam of white water was visible where the water churned over the rocks in the centre of the river.

'You have to be joking, Beck,' said Marco. 'We haven't a chance against a current like that.'

But Beck had already made up his mind. 'Tarzan's little helper to the rescue,' he muttered as he hacked at the root of a vine winding around the colossal trunk of a nearby tree. Cutting it free, he wrapped the vine around his shoulder like a climbing rope. Then he knelt down next to the twins as if he were a commando giving a briefing before a raid.

'We'll use the vine like a looped rope,' he said. 'I'll tie myself to it and cross first. Marco, Chrissy, you hold onto the rope on the bank but stand about three metres apart. That means I've got two anchors if I slip or fall. Then, when I'm over, Chrissy, you tie yourself onto it and we'll be anchoring you from both banks. Then, when Marco crosses, we'll both be on the far side. That way everyone has two anchors at all times.'

Beck tied the vine around his waist and waded slowly into the torrent. As the water began to rise around his legs, the twins braced themselves hard against the bank, ready to take the strain if he slipped. 'Face upstream and lean forward on your stick against the current,' Beck shouted. 'That way your legs and the stick are like a tripod. It's much more stable.' By the time he reached the far bank, the twins could hardly hear his voice above the roar of the water.

'He's ready for you, sis,' Marco said, once Beck was safe on dry land and had given the thumbs-up.

Christina waded into the swirling water. Almost at once her legs began to feel like jelly, and as the force of the current took hold, she fought to keep her balance on the uneven floor of the river bed.

'It's too strong,' she screamed back to Marco over the roar of the water. 'I can hardly move.'

Marco urged her onwards from the bank, shouting words of encouragement at every step as she slowly edged forward. Beck looked on nervously, the vine wrapped around his body and his hands gripping firmly as he dug his feet into the bank, preparing to take the strain if Christina was sucked away.

She was soon taking the full force of the river. After nearly losing her balance in the middle, where the current was at its strongest, she could at last feel the water getting shallower as she edged towards the far side. Sensing safety, she took a big stride forward, putting all her weight on the surface of a flat rock. In an instant, she was gone. Her foot went from under her on the slippery surface, and the current was immediately dragging her down and the foaming water smothering her face.

But Beck and Marco were ready for her. Digging their feet into the banks, they took the full weight of her body as the vine locked around her. Beck saw the danger at once. The water was rising in a wave around Christina's face and her head was being sucked under by the force of the water. He started running downstream, yelling at Marco to do the same. In an instant the tension was released and

Christina's head bobbed up again as she struggled to regain her balance, coughing water from her mouth.

Seeing his chance, Beck pulled on the vine with all his strength as Marco let more length slip through his fingers, and Christina was dragged, spluttering towards the bank.

CHAPTER 31

'That was a little too close for comfort,' said Beck later as they all sat drying out around the crackling warmth of a fire. Beck had been carrying the burning charcoal in the Kogi bag and had fanned it expertly back into life. Even he was impressed that it had kept smouldering inside its bark envelope during the difficult river crossing.

When the fire was well-stoked, Beck grabbed the sweetcorn from the Kogi bag and soon had it roasting over the flames. Soon they sat munching greedily as the juice from the cobs dribbled down their chins. But Beck was worried. All three of them were wet and exhausted. And ahead of them lay a long, steep climb as the jungle rose into the mountains above them. But somewhere up there, now surely only a day's walk away, lay the goal they had fought so hard to reach.

He let the twins rest as long as he dared. Finally he stood up and kicked out the remains of the fire, taking care to preserve another smouldering stick in the bark envelope. Even if it went out, it would be far easier to light again than fresh wood from the forest. 'One last effort, guys. Marco, Chrissy, we've come so far. We can't give up now. Remember, it's not for us, it's for them. Your dad and Uncle Al are depending on us.'

High in the trees above them, Ringo suddenly appeared and gave a squawk of agreement. The twins slowly hauled themselves to their feet, and a look of grim determination passed between them.

Following the banks of the river, which fell away into a canyon beside them, they made slow and painful progress upwards, zigzagging back and forth across the face of the slope to ease the pressure on their legs. In places they found themselves scrambling up almost sheer cliffs covered with the gnarled roots of trees, and were forced to make long detours into the jungle.

At last the river gorge began to narrow and a series of waterfalls plunged into the ravine like the tiers of a wedding cake. The temperature too had begun to drop as the day wore on and they climbed ever higher. 'It seems to be levelling out now and the jungle's not quite so thick,' said Marco as, late in the afternoon, they stopped to rest.

Checking for snakes before clearing a space on the jungle floor, Beck spread out the map in front of them. 'According to Gonzalo, the ceremonial path to the Lost City runs down to the edge of the plateau not far from the river. It just has to be so close to where we are now.' He pointed to where a line snaked across the parchment. Alongside it were written the words *Via Indígena* in a faded, spidery hand.

Beck shouted instructions as, spreading out, they walked slowly forward in a line, scraping the floor of the jungle with their sticks.

'It's got to be here somewhere,' muttered Marco, a note of desperation in his voice, when after an hour of searching they had still found nothing.

'Beck! Marco!' Christina was kicking something next to her foot and scraping excitedly at the moss on the jungle floor. In a moment the boys were by her side. The edge of a carved block of stone was clearly visible. Alongside it lay another stone of identical size and shape. Nearby, still more had been forced up out of the ground by the twisting roots of an old tree.

Marco was soon on his feet, looking backwards and forwards along the floor of the jungle. 'The Kogi path. This must be the Kogi path!' The energy and determination had returned to his voice. There was no mistaking it now: they were standing on the jumbled remains of an ancient stone causeway.

Beck slowly led the way forward. They could hear the roar of the canyon in the distance and the leaves were dripping in a permanent mist where the spray from the river engulfed the surrounding jungle.

Beck was thinking hard. It still made no sense. Gonzalo's map showed the path running parallel with the canyon, not across it. That's why they'd risked everything to cross lower down. Then he remembered the story Kojek had told him. After

Gonzalo had found their sacred city, the Kogis had abandoned it and redirected the paths through the forest to confuse the conquistadors if they returned. Did that mean the path marked on Gonzalo's map was wrong? So, was *this* the path leading to the Lost City? If so, it was heading back towards the gorge.

With a sinking sensation in his stomach, Beck led the way forward as the roar of the river became ever louder. After a while they could hardly hear each other speak above the din. Beck's heart was thumping. Their mission to find Uncle Al and Mayor Rafael was crumbling before them. They had fallen into the same trap as Gonzalo and now there was no way forward. Crossing the river this high in the mountains would surely be impossible.

As the path approached the edge, Beck could just make out the sheer rock face on the opposite side of the gorge. Where the remains of the path reached the cliff, a series of thick vines hung down from the branches of the trees to where a bridge had been suspended across the canyon. It sagged alarmingly over the abyss. Moving carefully closer, they stared down. Far below them, the waterfall pounded onto the rocks, sending jets of spray high into the air.

'Kojek's people must have built this,' shouted Beck above the roar of the torrent. 'But it can't have been used for years.'

He was interrupted by a raucous bellow and a hideous screeching in the trees above them. Christina grimaced and put her hands over her ears. The bellow came again. Then the branches began to shake violently and suddenly dozens of eyes were staring down at them.

'It's a troop of red howler monkeys,' he shouted. 'Best to get over the river as soon as we can. They could be dangerous if they start hurling branches down at us. Those tails of theirs are like having a third arm. And the other two could knock out the world heavyweight champ. In the first round.'

He turned away and looked down into the canyon. 'There's no way that bridge is strong enough to take all of us at once. We'll have to cross one at a time.'

Marco looked up to see a huge gaping mouth and a pair of flaring nostrils above him as another ear-splitting shriek rose above the roar of the river. The creature was covered in a thick mat of flame-red hair and crouched menacingly in the branches above.

The light was beginning to fade now and there was no time to lose. 'The moment I'm safe on the other side, follow me,' Beck shouted back at the twins. 'But don't start until I'm well clear.'

He started to edge out over the abyss. The bridge was slippery and treacherous and his hands clung tightly to the vines on either side as he made his way slowly forward. Through the lattice of vines beneath his feet, he could see the water thundering onto the rocks far below.

By the time he had reached the lowest point of the bridge and begun hauling himself back up again towards the cliff face on the far side, the bridge was swaying alarmingly. But the edge of the cliff was now almost within reach.

Then, without warning, the largest of the howler monkeys swung himself out by his tail from the trees above where the twins were crouching. For a moment he seemed to hang in mid-air above the gorge before he threw out a lanky arm and grabbed the side of the bridge behind Beck.

Clinging to the vines, he began leaping up and down in a frenzy, screeching and barking. He was followed by another monkey, and then another, until the whole troop were swinging from the bridge. As it shook violently beneath him, Beck clung grimly to the sides to stop himself being catapulted into the chasm below. Behind him, he could hear the twins screaming in vain at the howler monkeys.

But it was already too late.

The bridge was collapsing under his feet.

CHAPTER 32

Beck was plunging into the abyss. Adrenalin surged through his veins as the blurred walls of the canyon rushed up beside him and he hurtled towards the rocks below. Then, as the bridge swung down beneath him, he made one last, desperate lunge.

The jolt punched the air clean out of his lungs. His arm had hooked itself around the final step of the bridge, which was still attached to the cliff edge, and his body shuddered to a halt. Now just one thin length of vine was all that lay between him and certain death on the rocks below.

Beck clung on for dear life. The howler monkeys were clambering up the remains of the bridge above him, screeching and barking as they dragged themselves onto the edge of the cliff. Beck scrabbled desperately for a foothold on the canyon wall as the remains of the bridge swung back and forth above the abyss and the spray thundered around him.

But his head was clearing now. Somewhere, deep inside him, he could hear his father's voice calling him from far off. That same calm voice that had given him courage when he first learned to climb as a boy. He closed his eyes as his mind shut out the thunder of the water crashing on the rocks beneath. 'For you, Dad,' Beck whispered. 'For you, I promise I will survive.'

Slowly he began the long strength-sapping task of pulling himself upwards, hand over hand. All other thoughts were gone now. Survival was all that mattered. The next vine, the next handhold, step by painful step he dragged himself upwards. At last the cliff edge was getting nearer and the overhanging undergrowth was nearly within reach. But Beck's last remaining ounce of strength was draining out of his exhausted body. The screaming of the howler monkeys above him had reached fever pitch. How puny, they mocked, were the efforts of this hairless ape clinging so desperately to life.

Then, with one final superhuman effort, Beck pulled himself up over the overhang and onto the top of the cliff. Lungs heaving, he crawled into the safety of the undergrowth. The roar of the water was muffled now and his heart was thumping like an express train. On the far side of the canyon, through the billowing spray, he could just make out the crouched figures of the twins. Marco was shouting over the roar of the water. 'You're going to have to go alone, Beck. We'll wait for you here.'

Beck smiled across at them. Then, as if someone else were guiding him, Beck felt his hand moving to his chest. Hands shaking, he pulled the amulet of the toad from under his shirt and held it up to where the last rays of the sun were breaking through the spray. Its eyes glinted across the canyon, flashing at the twins.

There was no option but for him to go on. It was up to him alone now. Somehow he would reach the Lost City and find Uncle Al and Mayor Rafael. And somehow he would outwit the gang and release them. If he could survive this, he could survive anything. Marco and Christina would have to use all the knowledge he had taught them and wait to be rescued. Somehow, he would make it back to them as soon as he could.

Beck tucked the amulet under his shirt again and took a last fleeting look back across the canyon. The twins were waving back at him now. Marco had a broad smile on his face and was pumping both hands above his head with fists clenched, as if urging an exhausted marathon runner across the line. Christina had put her fingers to her lips and was blowing him a kiss across the gorge.

After one more glance back, Beck dragged himself away from the cliff edge. Summoning all his willpower, he hacked a trail through the dense foliage. He was thankful that he'd been carrying the machete – though he worried how the twins would manage without it. He could still just make out the route of the Kogi path where it led away from the bridge into the jungle. In the trees above him, the bellows of the howler monkeys grew ever louder as the roar of the waterfall dwindled behind him. By now, the last remaining daylight was beginning to fade and the tropical night was closing in once more.

CHAPTER 33

Beck's mind began to wander as he dragged his exhausted body onwards. Just a few short weeks ago he had been the captain of his victorious school rugby team, looking forward to an exotic trip with Uncle Al. Back home, spring would be in the air and his friends preparing for the cricket season. The thought tugged at his heartstrings. He could smell the aroma of linseed oil and hear the sound of cricket spikes on the steps of the pavilion as he made his way out to bat. The crowd were shouting his name and—

His reverie was rudely interrupted. The gruff voice of his sergeant major on cadet training in the Highlands of Scotland was booming inside his head. '*Any fool can be uncomfortable, Granger,*' it bellowed. '*Easiest thing in the world. Just lie down in a ditch and feel sorry for yourself. Forget your shelter. No water, no fire, no food. Just close your eyes. And you'll never wake up again . . .*'

Suddenly Beck was wide awake. The sergeant major's voice had dissolved into the bark of the howler monkeys in the trees above him. Their howls were becoming ever more threatening and they bared their teeth, as if they blamed him for having ended up stranded on the wrong side of the canyon.

But Beck's head was clearing again now. He knew only too well the tricks the mind could play in the final stages of exhaustion. If he let himself sleep now, the warm blanket of death would soon wash over him . . . No he had to keep moving.

Beck groaned. Deep inside he knew that unless he could shake himself free of his stupor now, he was done for. He had no choice but to make camp exactly where he was. He needed to get warm fast if he were to survive the night. He felt for the familiar shape of the fire steel on the lace around his neck and quickly went to work.

Night had fallen by the time the fire was at last

ablaze. Frightened by the flames, the howler moneys had melted away and the familiar calls of the jungle had returned. For the first time since the bridge collapsed, Beck had stopped shivering. By the light of the flames, he cut himself another stick with the machete and quickly cleared the debris from the jungle floor. With his last remaining strength, he built a simple sleeping platform of bare branches laid together to keep himself clear of the stinging, biting creatures on the ground beneath. It was hardly the comfort the sergeant major had in mind, but it would have to do.

As the flames burned lower, Beck at last allowed himself to sink into sleep. His dreams were troubled from the start. Uncle Al appeared, riding a golden toad whose croak sounded like the hideous bark of the howler monkeys. They were being chased by the sleek, dark shape of a huge cat skulking in the shadows, its eyes shining bright as diamonds. Beck felt the eyes boring into him, but when he raised his eyes to meet them, he was back in the square in Cartagena once more. The face of Mama Kojek hung over him.

He woke with a start. There was a commotion above his head and the sound of sticks smashing into the ground beside him. In the watery gloom of morning his tormentors had returned and he could see the faces of the howler monkeys peering down at him from the trees. Beck cursed. Barking and howling too, he hurled whatever missiles he could find back up at them. Within minutes he was exhausted.

But in the cold light of morning, Beck's mind was clearer. During the night he had woken several times to hear the snarl of the jaguar stalking in the jungle somewhere nearby. Each time, the heart-numbing growl came from a different direction. And each time, it seemed to come closer. Now he lay still. His mind was working fast. This was no time for mistakes or wrong decisions. If the howler monkeys followed him for much longer, they would surely attract the attention of the jaguar.

There was only one chance. Playing dead was not a survival strategy Beck would normally use. Especially with a bumptious group of young howler monkeys. Once, in the African bush, he had been thrown from a horse when his party disturbed a lion sleeping in the undergrowth. Playing dead that day had saved his life. When he felt the lion's hot breath on his neck, his heart almost stopped beating. Finally it had stalked off.

Beck did the same now. Hoping against hope that the jaguar had feasted well during the night and was now sleeping off his meal, he lay still as the monkeys screeched and cried above him. Surely they would grow tired and leave this hairless ape alone. During the night Beck had clutched at Gonzalo's amulet, the eyes of the Indian burning inside his head.

Finally, just as Beck was giving up hope that the monkeys would ever leave, their howls began to fade. The shaking and squealing in the branches above his head had stopped and the hail of missiles had dwindled to a trickle. As their calls slowly receded into the distance, Beck let out a long, low sigh of relief.

But Beck, by now, was exhausted, utterly drained of energy. He was struggling just to stand. He was dehydrated, cold, wet, sleep-deprived and at his wits' end.

Then, hardly knowing what he was doing, he felt his fingers groping for the amulet from under his shirt. And for the first time since his dream he put the toad to his lips.

And blew.

CHAPTER 34

When Beck came to, he guessed it was around midday. He got to his feet and started to walk, following the Kogis' path once more through the jungle. The howler monkeys were nowhere to be seen and the undergrowth was becoming less dense. Above him the trees were getting taller, and as the day wore on, he caught glimpses of blue through the clouds high above him. The carved stones of the path were growing easier to make out under the lichen and moss.

By now, Beck's instinct for survival was on auto-pilot. In front of him he moved his stick from side to side like a zombie with a metal detector. As long as the Kogi path lay under his feet, he knew that sooner or later he would find the Lost City. But his mind was starting to wander once more.

His thoughts returned to the twins. Where were they now? Had they managed to make a camp? He knew Marco still had the embers in the fire sleeve. With any luck, they would have been able to make a fire to keep themselves warm during the night. He thought of Christina and the look in her eyes when she had blown that kiss across the river. He wondered whether—

He stopped suddenly. His stick had hit something hard on the floor of the jungle. Immediately all thoughts of the twins were gone. The path seemed to have suddenly run into a brick wall. For a moment he stood rooted to the spot, unable to believe what his senses were telling him. Then he remembered: the words and numbers that had made no sense the day they discovered Gonzalo's map at the hacienda. Beck spread out the map in front of him. Next to the scrawled figure of a toad were the words *Escalera con mil pasos*. A staircase with a thousand steps.

Beck slowly raised his eyes and looked up. Ahead, disappearing into the distance, was a stone staircase that seemed to be leading up the side of a huge mountain into the clouds. It was covered in a carpet of green – in places the roots of trees wrapped around the steps like gnarled fingers.

Beck took a deep breath and began to climb.

1, 2, 3 . . .

He felt as if he were climbing the steps of a great cathedral. In the eerie light of the forest, the atmosphere was overpowering. Huge vines, bigger than any Beck had yet seen, hung down around him. Above, the branches of giant trees arched over the ceremonial steps like the swords of a guard of honour.

148, 149, 150 . . .

As he climbed higher, peering into the gloom on either side of the giant staircase, he could make out the remains of ancient terraces and stone fireplaces where the houses of the ancient Kogis had once stood.

373, 374, 375 . . .

Pausing for a moment to rest, Beck wiped the sweat from his brow. Suddenly the sun burst through the trees high above and the shadow of a giant cat towered over him. He cowered helplessly, waiting for the giant talons to rip into his flesh. But it was frozen in mid-pounce, its shadow etched on the steps in front of him. Slowly Beck raised his head. Choked by the vegetation, the jaguar was carved from solid stone.

As the shock gradually drained from his body, Beck could make out statues in the undergrowth all around him. The wings of a giant condor. The fangs of a snake. The tail of a monkey. The city felt as if it had been frozen in time; as if some demon of the mountains had turned all the creatures of the jungle to stone.

488, 489, 500 . . .

Beck stopped. And listened. He was halfway to the top now, and doubting voices inside his head were crowding in on him like the dark shadows of the jungle itself. Now that he had come so far, would all his efforts be in vain? What would he do if he came face to face with the kidnappers? How would he rescue Uncle Al and Mayor Rafael? He put his right hand across his body and felt for the handle of the machete. From now on, he would need to be as quiet as the grave.

748, 749, 750 . . .

Beck was climbing slowly now, crouching down among the statues in the shadows beside the staircase. His eyes flicked nervously from side to side, scanning the jungle. High above him he could see the outlines of curving stone walls buried in the undergrowth. Centuries ago, ancient Kogi craftsmen must have built these ceremonial platforms. But since the city had been deserted, huge trees had smothered them with their roots like the tentacles of a giant squid.

973, 974, 975 . . .

The steps were narrowing now and the ground was beginning to level out. Beck peered into a narrow passage between two huge walls that towered above him. Ahead, a stone archway linked two ceremonial platforms standing on either side of the staircase. Thick tangles of foliage hung down from the crumbling stone arch like a curtain.

988, 989, 990 . . .

A sudden screech made Beck jump out of his skin. A blur of coloured feathers swooped from the branches of an overhanging tree. It was Ringo. The parakeet was soon flapping his wings and squawking at Beck for all he was worth from his perch on top of the archway.

Beck froze. The back of his neck felt cold and goose pimples ran down his spine. Then he heard a sound like a boot scraping against stone and the faint pop of a twig snapping. It was followed by another outburst from Ringo. Beck tightened his grip on the handle of his machete and continued up towards the archway.

997, 998, 999 . . .

Beck stopped again and listened. He could feel his heart thumping in his chest and blood pounding at his temples. He put his foot on the final step of the staircase. Slowly he raised the machete towards the curtain of vines that hung from the arch and gently parted them with the tip of the blade.

There, under the archway, in a stone chair like the throne of a medieval king, sat a hooded figure shrouded in darkness. Two glittering eyes stared out at Beck. His heart leaped. Was he safe at last? Had Kojek heard the call of the amulet and been following them all along?

1,000 . . .

As Beck moved forward under the arch to greet Kojek, two burly figures leaped out of the shadows beside him and grabbed him, pinning his arms roughly behind his back.

The figure in the stone chair rose slowly to his feet.

Then it spoke.

'*Buenos días, amigo*,' snarled Ramirez.

Beck's legs buckled under him and he collapsed.

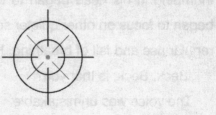

CHAPTER 35

Beck's head was thumping and bright lights like laser beams bored into his head. His mind was a blur and he was struggling to remember where he was.

He could feel hard rock under him and his limbs ached. Every time he tried to move, the lights flashed brighter, his head thumped harder. As he attempted to raise his arm to rub his aching head, he felt the sharp steel of handcuffs digging into his wrists.

Struggling to sit upright, he let out a long agonized groan. A blindfold had been tied too tightly around his eyes and was digging into his temples. The sound of dripping water echoed in his ears and there was a smell of dampness in the air. At last the thumping in his head began to slow and his mind began to focus on other quieter sounds nearby. The regular rise and fall of breathing. He was not alone.

'Beck. Beck, is that you?'

The voice was unmistakable.

'Uncle Al?'

'Beck. Beck, my boy. What are you doing here?' Uncle Al's voice was trembling with emotion. Beck felt tears welling up in his eyes. He tried to speak but his uncle and Mayor Rafael were both talking at once. A flood of questions washed over him. Was he all right? Were the twins with him? How had he found them? Was there a rescue party on its way?

In between spasms of relief and despair, Beck tried to explain everything as best he could. Mayor Rafael gasped in amazement when he told them the story of Gonzalo's map and the golden toad. Then Beck explained how they had escaped from under the noses of Ramirez's men and described their voyage down the coast aboard the *Bella Señora* and the shipwreck near the Kogi village.

At last both men fell silent as Beck told them the story of Kojek, and his discovery of the true story behind Gonzalo's golden amulet. Mayor Rafael let out a stifled cry when Beck explained how the twins had been left stranded on the other side of the river when the Kogi bridge had collapsed. A hushed silence fell once again when he told them about the final disastrous encounter with Ramirez.

At last Mayor Rafael spoke.

'Ramirez has been planning this for years. He was always asking questions about Gonzalo. Once he realized I was setting up an expedition to find the Lost City, he knew he had to act or his chance would be gone.'

'How did you know where to find the city without Gonzalo's map?' asked Beck.

'I've known about the map for years,' said the mayor. 'A few weeks ago I finally discovered the hiding place, but it was too dangerous to let anyone know. It was a secret even from Maria and the twins. But when I heard that Professor Granger was in the country, I knew the time was right to mount an exped-ition. If we could discover the Lost City, the looters would have lost their chance. But I hadn't reckoned on Ramirez. That was my big mistake.'

'So you told Ramirez where to find the city?' asked Beck.

'I didn't tell him about the map. But I had already hired porters and a team to make the expedition into the jungle. One of them was in Ramirez's pay. So he knew I had a good idea where the city was, if not how I knew. All that was needed then was to stage a kidnapping and make it look like he had nothing to do with it. After that terrible night in the square, we were held in a prison cell by Ramirez until I agreed to help him find the city.'

Beck heard a stifled cough, as if the mayor were choking back tears.

'I was so worried about what he might do to Maria and the twins. I had no choice.'

'So how did you find the city?' asked Beck. 'And how did you get here?'

'No one believed it could be reached by sea,' Mayor Rafael continued. 'The mountains are too sheer and the jungle too thick. It is a miracle you managed to survive. I believed that the only way in was from the other side of the mountain. Ramirez's men have a helicopter base there. It's officially for hunting the drug barons and destroying their crops. So once Ramirez had forced the information out of me, it was easy. The police have infra-red cameras and they scanned the jungle for days. Finally they found it and we were dropped off by helicopter.'

A heavy silence fell, broken only by the sullen dripping of water from the roof of their prison. Then Uncle Al was speaking again.

'Beck, we are all in great danger. Once Ramirez has found the gold, he plans to kill us. Kidnappings happen every day in Colombia. People disappear for months, sometimes years. Ramirez will keep up his smoke screen. If our bodies are recovered, he will simply blame the drug barons.'

Beck was fighting despair. They had survived against all the odds and now it had come to this. He was mumbling about how they mustn't lose hope for the twins' sake and how they would find a way—

Then a blinding headache suddenly crept up on him and everything went black.

In the darkness he lost all track of time. His nightmares returned. He was back in the burning Kogi village: screaming women and children scattered around him, desperately trying to escape the slashing swords of Gonzalo's conquistadors. Once more he was gazing into the eyes of the golden toad . . . Which in turn changed into the reptilian eyes of Ramirez . . . Which in turn changed into the eyes of Kojek . . . Which were now turning—

He woke with a jolt. There was a sound of boots on stone and someone shoved him hard in the ribs. Two voices were raised in anger and there was a quick exchange in Spanish. Mayor Rafael let out a stifled laugh. 'Ramirez can't find any gold. All this – and for what?'

His words were followed by a curse Beck heard the sickening thump of a boot crunching into the mayor's stomach. He flinched as the mayor let out an anguished scream that echoed around the cave.

And now Beck was being dragged to his feet.

'*Vamos, Inglés,*' hissed a voice in his ear as he was pushed roughly forwards.

'Be brave, Beck, my boy!' Uncle Al's echoing voice faded behind him as he was bundled out of the room. After sitting down for so long, Beck almost fainted as the blood rushed from his pounding head. He could see shafts of sunlight through his blindfold – their angle, along with the smell of the jungle, told him that it was already evening. Men were shouting to each other in Spanish and he could hear the ringing clink of metal on stone and smell the odour of freshly dug earth.

He was being pushed up a series of stone steps, and when he slipped and stumbled, he was dragged roughly to his feet again. Then he was brought to a halt and someone started fumbling with his wrists as his handcuffs were unlocked. His hands were numb and he felt a stab of pain in his fingers as the blood rushed back into them.

The next minute his blindfold was removed. Beck blinked and gazed around. Mountain peaks circled him on all sides. It was almost dark now and a glowing ember of orange light was dropping over the horizon as a blood-red sunset lit up the sky. He was standing on one of the high, circular terraces he had seen when he was climbing the staircase of a thousand steps, and was now looking out over the jungle canopy below. Searchlights lit up the night sky, and around him men were scanning the ground with metal detectors and digging into the soft earth.

But something else caught Beck's eye. The outline of a huge rock was silhouetted against the red sunset. It stood to one side of the terrace on its own simple platform. There was no mistaking that familiar outline. He had first seen it bobbing above the crowds at the carnival in Cartagena, then on the coat of arms of the mayor's family crest and finally in Gonzalo's golden amulet.

He remembered Kojek's words. This was surely none other than *la rana*, the toad stone, the ancient goddess of the Kogis. And quietly sitting on its head between the two raised discs of its bulbous eyes was Ringo.

'*Buenos días, amigo.*'

CHAPTER 36

Beck spun round. Ramirez was staring at him with a look of undisguised malice. He barked an order and the two men who had bundled him out of his prison began frisking him. One of the men gave a shout and the belt carrying Gonzalo's map was roughly pulled out from around his waist. A satisfied smile crossed the police chief's face. Studying it briefly, he handed it back to the men, who started pointing out over the terraces and shouting orders to the men digging below.

But Beck could not help himself now. He felt nothing but contempt for Ramirez. '*Oro no más*,' he spat. 'The gold is gone.' As soon as the words were out of his mouth, Beck wished he had stayed silent. In a fit of rage Ramirez strode towards him and, grabbing him around the neck, lifted him clean off the ground.

The moment the policeman's fist closed around his shirt, Beck knew it was all over. A ghastly smile spread over Ramirez's lips. Feeling Gonzalo's amulet under Beck's shirt, he slowly lowered him to the ground.

'*El oro de Gonzalo, por favor*,' he said quietly, motioning to Beck to remove the amulet from around his neck.

Beck knew he had no choice. Slowly undoing the top button of his shirt, he lifted the golden toad from around his neck, letting it swing slowly from side to side in front of the police chief's face.

Ramirez's face was twisted in a ghastly smile, as if he had been hypnotized by the amulet: his eyes followed it back and forth. '*La rana!*' he whispered, almost laughing. '*El oro de la rana!*'

Suddenly, his words were drowned out by a screech and a loud beat of wings. Ramirez was flailing at something above his head and feathers were flying all around him. Beck did not miss his chance. As Ringo dive-bombed the policeman,

Beck grabbed the amulet from Ramirez, put it to his lips, and blew.

In an instant a ring of fire burst into life on the terraces below – flaming torches rose out of the jungle on all sides. Ramirez's men looked at each other in horror. Ramirez snatched the amulet from Beck and kicked him to the ground. Ramirez's men were now shouting and running in all directions on the surrounding terraces in blind panic.

Beck got to his feet and, seizing his chance, he dived over the edge of the terrace and made a run for cover. Above him, silhouetted against the sky, Beck could see Ramirez pulling a gun out of a holster at his waist. Leaping onto the platform with the toad stone, the police chief was soon scrabbling desperately at the ground beneath, a mad glint in his cruel eyes.

Beck watched in amazement as a sea of Kogi figures surged up out of the jungle, lit by the blazing torches. The ring of fire was rising up on all sides, as if every tree in the forest were ablaze. Beck gazed down the staircase of a thousand steps. The statues on either side seemed almost alive, as if all the animals of the jungle were glistening in the firelight, willing the Kogis along.

And then Beck's heart leaped. For at the top of the stairs under the ceremonial arch Beck spotted Kojek, his eyes glittering. Then his heart skipped a beat once more, for there, just a few steps behind him, were Marco and Christina.

Beck let out a shout and burst from his cover. He was soon hugging the twins at the top of the steps as the Kogis crowded around the three joyful teenagers. In front of them, Kojek stood under the archway. For the first time Beck could remember, the merest hint of a smile softened his stern features.

And then, in the blink of an eye, it happened. One of Ramirez's men shouted a warning from above, and as everyone turned to look, a dark feline shape emerged from the depths of the jungle on the far side of the terraces. The creature moved so fast that to Beck it was like a shadow passing over the face of the moon. Like a coiled spring, it leaped from terrace to terrace, and in just a few strides it was closing on its prey.

An ear-piercing scream tore through the jungle

night as the teeth of the jaguar crunched into Ramirez's skull. It was followed by a deep rumbling growl as the creature rose up on its hind legs, snarling in triumph at the moon.

A slow trickle of blood was dripping onto the staircase of a thousand steps.

Ramirez was dead.

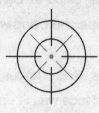

CHAPTER 37

Beck was standing once more at the foot of the great staircase. The twins were with him. Above them, stretching up towards the archway high above, Kogis with blazing firebrands lined the steps. The statues of the jungle animals had been roughly cleared of vegetation and formed a guard of honour beside them. Eerie shadows flickered in the inky darkness as the jungle canopy closed in above them.

Earlier that evening, after Ramirez's men had either surrendered or fled into the jungle, there had been a tearful and joyful reunion with Uncle Al and the twins' father. When they had all finally recovered, Mayor Rafael found a high-frequency radio on Ramirez's body and spoke to one of his staff in the mayoral office in Cartagena. A rescue party had been despatched, and would be with them imminently.

'I think Kojek is ready for us,' said a voice in Beck's ear. Marco's face was lit up in a broad smile.

'Time for the Younger Brother to make amends,' said Christina on his other side.

They heard a loud screech. Beck turned to see Ringo perched on Mayor Rafael's shoulder behind them. Uncle Al stood to one side, looking at the bird inquisitively.

'I'm sorry. I don't think you've been introduced,' said Beck. 'Uncle Al, Ringo. Ringo, Uncle Al.'

'Jolly nice to meet you, Ringo,' said Uncle Al, grinning broadly and stretching out his hand.

Ringo tilted his head, eyeing the stranger suspiciously before gingerly stretching out a claw and gripping one of Uncle Al's fingers.

'Uncle Al, Ringo. Ringo, Uncle Al,' screeched Ringo loudly. Uncle Al raised his panama hat, smiling.

'Well, at least he's remembered how to talk again,' said Marco. 'All he's done is screech ever since we arrived in the jungle.'

And now the small group began the long climb towards the archway above. Beck led the way, Gonzalo's amulet hanging proudly on its gold chain around his neck. At each step, as they climbed ever higher, the Kogis on each side made a small bow of welcome. When at last they reached the archway, Kojek rose to greet them. One by one, they stepped forward and bowed to him in turn.

When they had finished, Kojek began to speak, his bright eyes shimmering in the torchlight.

'The Elder Brother greets the Younger Brother. It is time to make things right.'

Then Mayor Rafael stepped forward. 'Kojek,' he replied in a strong, clear voice. 'My ancestor came to this place many centuries ago and took something that is rightfully yours. Today we are proud to return it to you.'

Beck led the way forward, following Kojek onto the terraces above. They were soon standing in front of the familiar outline of *la rana,* the Toad Stone.

And now at last Kojek's lips began moving as he started to chant in the Kogi tongue. All the Kogis who had greeted them on the steps below gathered around them in a great circle, their torches lighting up the night. The sound of the chanting seemed to Beck as if it were coming from the bowels of the earth.

He was standing behind Kojek now, with the twins on either side. 'Chrissy,' he whispered suddenly. 'Before we do this, there's something I want to give you.'

The twins looked at Beck with shocked expressions on their faces, as if he had been caught talking during a church service given by the Pope in St Peter's in Rome.

Beck was fumbling for something in his pocket and at last produced a dirty-looking rag. 'I forgot to give you these back.'

Christina took the damp piece of cotton from Beck's hand and slowly opened it. Inside, two gold question marks glinted in the torchlight. Christina gave Beck a quick hug just as Kojek turned to address them once more.

'Children of the Younger Brother. You have come here with a gift.'

Beck and the twins stepped forward to where a

small alcove had been dug in the earth beneath *la rana*. The chanting around them rose to a crescendo. Beck took the golden amulet from around his neck and, with the twins on either side, stepped forward and lowered it into the darkness beneath.

Then he turned and gazed deep into Kojek's eyes.

'*Perdido no más*,' he said.

The amulet was finally home.

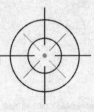

TYING KNOTS

In chapter 18 of *Gold of the Gods*, Beck uses a bowline knot to make sure his machete isn't lost overboard during a shark attack. Tying knots is one of the most useful skills you can learn for when you're out in the wild. Here are a few of Bear's top knots:

Bowline

This is probably the most useful knot you'll ever learn. It's used to form a loop at the end of a rope. It can be tied very quickly and it won't slip or tighten. There's a useful mnemonic you can use to remember how to tie it.

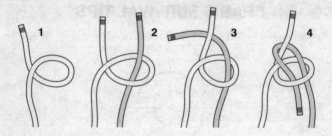

1) The rabbit hole **2)** The rabbit comes out **3)** It runs round the tree **4)** It goes back down its hole

If your life depends on a bowline, add a half hitch in the working end when finished. This makes it a hundred per cent secure.

Clove hitch

Use this to attach a rope to a horizontal pole or post.

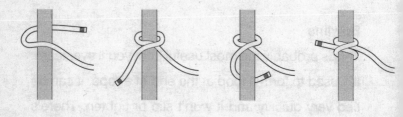

Constrictor knot

This is really useful for tying the neck of a bag or sack.

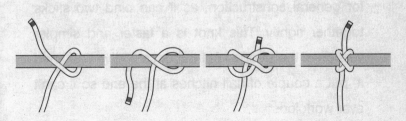

Figure of 8 loop

This knot is easy to learn, reliable and – crucially for a good knot – easy to untie. It is a very popular knot with climbers and sailors, but you can bet you'll find a use for it in the field. It is particularly useful when the final loop can be passed over a post.

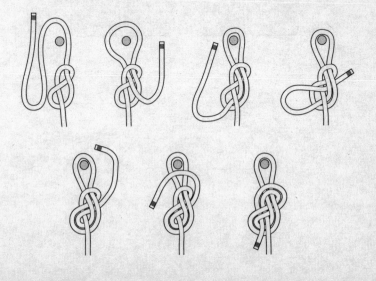

Jam knot

Also known as the locking knot, this is a good knot for general construction, as it can bind two sticks together tightly. This knot is a faster and simpler version of the sledge knot but once you've tightened it, put a couple of half hitches at the end so it can't ever work loose.

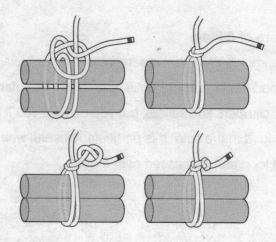

Beck Granger returns in . . .

Book 2:

WAY OF THE WOLF

Read on for a sneak preview . . .

CHAPTER 1

The small plane crawled across the landscape like an insect over a tablecloth.

Beck Granger peered out at the patchwork of Alaskan wilderness thousands of feet below. It was spring and the thaw was all but complete. Not long ago it would have all been a smooth white, a land of ice and snow. Now he could see fir trees, grass, moss. Streams and rivers ran with crystal-clear meltwater. Endless shades of green, all tied together with fine silver threads.

Beck pressed his face to the window. He could just see the blur of the single propeller. The plane was a Cessna 180. Beck's Uncle Al, sitting in front next to the pilot, had told him it was the workhorse of the far north. It had a streamlined body like a plump fish suspended beneath its single wing. The cabin had a grand total of six seats, but at the moment there were only three passengers, plus the pilot. The back of the plane was stuffed with their bags and equipment.

Like everyone else on board, Beck was wearing large padded earphones. Without them the noise of the engine would have made talking to anyone impossible. Even with them on, the vibration rumbled like a tumbledryer in his guts.

A burst of static in his ears meant that the pilot had switched on the intercom.

'I'm adding an hour to the journey, guys.' She was a cheerful woman, middle-aged and stocky. You could see that she was descended from people who had made a home in this wilderness. 'There's bad weather ahead over the mountains and I intend to go right round it. It's way too much for this little plane.' The static went away again, and at the same time the plane began to tilt.

'OK,' Beck called, but he hadn't switched on his own intercom and his voice was lost in the roar of the engine.

The plane turned and brought the mountains into

view through the side windows. Beck looked out at them with respect. The thaw only reached part way up them. Maybe it never got higher. The trees grew part way up too, and then stopped abruptly in a ragged line, as if the mountains had shrugged them off as they burst from the ground. After that there was just grey rock clawing at the sky from beneath a thin white sheet of snow and ice.

The storm sat on top of the mountains like a wild creature feasting on the peaks, which were lost in a dark, whirling cloud. It was quite literally a force of nature: Beck could see why the pilot didn't want to risk her little plane against it. It was like coming across a bear in the wild. You didn't push your luck – you just took another route. That way everyone lived happily.

More static meant that the pilot was going to speak again.

'The good news is, the storm's not coming towards us. It's heading away but I don't want to catch it up. We're going to be a bit delayed doing this detour. I sure hope Anakat's worth it.'

'It will be,' Uncle Al promised. 'Trust me.'

CHAPTER 2

Anakat, their destination, lay on Alaska's west coast, looking out over the Bering Sea.

'I've stopped over there a couple of times,' the pilot continued. 'You know, the elders there have an oral tradition that goes back centuries. They can recite their entire history at the drop of a hat. They know this land inside out and back to front.'

'I can't wait to meet them,' Uncle Al agreed. He twisted round in his seat to wink at Beck. Beck smiled back. They both knew this wasn't just a pleasure trip.

Uncle Al didn't really make pleasure trips – all his travels had a point to them. To the rest of the world he was Professor Sir Alan Granger, anthropologist and TV personality with a keen interest in environmental matters. When they were alive, Beck's parents had taken him all over the world in their travels on behalf of Green Force, the environmental direct action group. Now Al was determined to carry on the good work of his younger brother, Beck's dad.

'With all due respect to the National Curriculum,' he had once said to Beck, 'you'll learn a lot more this way.'

That, as Beck recalled, had been as they flew out to the Australian Outback to live with a community of Aboriginals . . .

He gazed back at the landscape outside. It looked very different to the baked desert of Western Australia but in some way it was very similar. This too was a world where Mother Nature ruled. Her word was law. An unprepared human being would be swallowed up and never seen again. It looked beautiful, but it was harsh and hostile.

But a *prepared* human being . . . ah, that was very different. A prepared human being could live in harmony with nature down there and never want for anything. The Inuit – the people who lived up here in the northern latitudes – spread from Alaska to Greenland; they had been managing it for thousands of years. That was why things like the oral tradition and culture of Anakat were so important. You could never learn it through books or off the web. You had to *live* it.

Beck and Uncle Al had flown from London to Seattle in a brand-new, wide-body airliner. Seattle-Tacoma International Airport was like a small space-age city, sparkling and modern. Then they had caught a plane to Anchorage, smaller and more crowded. And finally they had been picked up by the Cessna for the four-hour flight out here, across a landscape that hadn't changed in thousands of years. With each stage of the journey, Beck had felt he was shedding something he didn't need; one more layer of the twenty-first century.

Someone tugged at his elbow. Beck turned away from the window to look at the plane's third passenger. The twenty-first century's greatest fan.

Tikaani was in the seat next to Beck's. Like Beck he was thirteen years old. His accent was pure American, but one look at his features and his sleek dark hair told you where his ancestry lay. He belonged to the Anak, one of the Inuit peoples native to this area. In fact Tikaani's father was the headman of Anakat. He was a forward-thinking man and had decided the village's isolation couldn't last. Someone had to go out and learn the ways of the modern world.

So Tikaani had been bundled off to school in Anchorage. When Beck and Uncle Al stopped off there, Al's contacts in Anakat had called and asked if they could pick up the boy for the last leg of their journey.

Rather than use the intercom, Tikaani just leaned close to Beck, pulled back the earphone and shouted.

'What are you looking at?'

Beck replied the same way, putting his head close to Tikaani's. 'This landscape!' he called. 'It's amazing!'

'Uh-huh . . .' Tikaani craned his neck to look out of Beck's window, but there was only polite interest on his face. He was just trying to be friendly. There wasn't anything down there he hadn't seen almost every day of his life. 'Right. Uh' – he waved the thin plastic sliver of Beck's iPod, which he had borrowed back in Anchorage – 'how do you make it shuffle?'

Beck fought the temptation to roll his eyes. He took the iPod gently out of Tikaani's hand and showed him how to scroll through the options on screen.

'Thanks!'

Tikaani sat back in his seat again. The iPod's thin wires disappeared inside the padding of his earphones. Beck smiled to himself and shook his head. Tikaani's father's plan to help his son learn the ways of the modern world had been a little too successful. For all Tikaani's Anak heritage, Beck suspected he would gladly drop the oral tradition and culture of Anakat down a deep dark hole and leave them there.

And perhaps he would get the chance, because his world was about to change in a way that even Tikaani's father had never dreamed of.

CHAPTER 3

Two years ago surveyors from the oil giant Lumos Petroleum had learned that Anakat sat slap-bang on top of a huge untapped oil field.

There had been village meetings to discuss the matter, of course – to discuss what to do when a multinational oil corporation wants to buy your ancestral land, destroy your way of life, relocate you . . . and sweetens the pill by offering every man, woman and child a brand-new home, with all modern amenities, and enough money in the bank to buy all the iPods you could ever want.

Beck knew that Tikaani, for one, was all in favour of it. He couldn't wait to be relocated. Among the adults of Anakat, the matter wasn't so clear cut. Even the money Lumos was offering didn't mean a lot to people who had never wanted much in the first place. It was that oral tradition again. They knew that what they could lose from their way of life was priceless in a way that Lumos's accountants would never understand.

And so Uncle Al was flying up to film a TV documentary about the village and the traditional Anak way of life. If it all changed, then at least there would be some record of it. Even better, the programme would make more people aware of just what was going on.

Suddenly there was a huge *BANG* and the plane lurched. Beck clutched at the armrests of his seat. The plane stabilized again; the engine was still running smoothly. Tikaani was sitting bolt upright, staring ahead, his face pale. Beck forced a smile. Wow! They must have hit an air pocket, and how! For a moment he had thought—

The engine stuttered and the plane shook. And then Beck realized that a trail of dark smoke was streaming past his window. It was coming from the engine. It grew thicker as he watched, from an innocuous wisp to an evil dark cloud in the freezing air outside.

And now the plane was very clearly banking to one side. It steadied again, but Beck could feel his insides lurching. The plane was dropping, and fast.

'Something's blown.' The pilot's calm tones in the earphones had gone, replaced with professional crispness. 'Oil feed's not getting through and engine temp's way up. I'm going to put the nose down and hope the air cools her enough to restart.'

Hope!? Beck wanted to scream. With the plane plummeting out of the sky, he could do with something a little more concrete than that . . .

The static went away and all that was left in Beck's ears was the roaring of his blood. The engine had stopped. No noise, no vibration. He pulled off the earphones. Air rushed past the plane's hull.

All he could see through the front windows was ground. Beck could hear the pilot's calm, urgent tones. 'Mayday, mayday, mayday. Anchorage, this is Golf Mike Oscar . . .'

'Beck . . .'

Beck barely heard. He was staring at the approaching trees. *This must have been what it was like—*

'*Beck!*' Uncle Al had turned in his seat again and his shout broke into Beck's reverie. 'And you too, Tikaani.'

Tikaani was also staring ahead like a mesmerized rabbit. Al had to click his fingers in front of the boy's face to get his attention.

'Both of you. You know the emergency position. Adopt it now.'

Beck and Tikaani glanced at each other, and then without a word they bent over double in their seats, arms wrapped around their knees, and waited. Beck had no idea what was going through Tikaani's head but his own thoughts continued to run away with him.

This must have been what it was like for Mum and Dad.

Three years earlier, they had been in a plane like this. It had crashed in the jungle. The plane had been found; they had not. They were presumed dead.

It had never occurred to Beck until now that a plane crash isn't instant. Something falling out of the sky takes time to reach the ground. And all you can do if you're on it is wait, and try not to picture the ground approaching . . .

The engine roared into life again and the pilot pulled back on the column. A mighty force pressed Beck back into his seat as the plane lifted. Tikaani shouted with triumph. Beck felt the plane levelling off, and lifted his head just in time to see trees rise up in front and smash into them.

BEAR GRYLLS is one of the world's most famous adventurers. After spending three years in the SAS he set off to explore the globe in search of even bigger challenges. He has climbed Mount Everest, crossed the Sahara Desert and circumnavigated Britain on a jet-ski. His TV shows have been seen by more than 1.2 billion viewers in more than 150 countries. In 2009, Bear became Chief Scout to the Scouting Association. He lives in London and Wales with his wife Shara and their three sons: Jesse, Marmaduke and Huckleberry.